"Who made you judge and jury of my morals?"

Anne spoke defiantly, but Tom seemed unmoved by her anger.

"I'm self-appointed. Anyone who flaunts herself the way you do and carries on as if no one else in the world matters deserves all she gets."

"You're talking about the past. It has nothing to do with the present," Anne said stiffly. "Anyway… what I do with my life is no concern of yours!"

Valerie Parv was a successful journalist and nonfiction writer when she began writing for Mills & Boon in 1982. Born in Shropshire, England, she grew up in Australia and now lives with her cartoonist husband and their cat—the office manager—in Sydney, New South Wales. She is a keen futurist and a "Star Trek" enthusiast, and her interests include traveling, restoring dollhouses and entertaining friends. Writing romance novels affirms her belief in love and happy endings.

Love Like Gold
Valerie Parv

Harlequin Books

TORONTO • NEW YORK • LONDON
AMSTERDAM • PARIS • SYDNEY • HAMBURG
STOCKHOLM • ATHENS • TOKYO • MILAN
MADRID • WARSAW • BUDAPEST • AUCKLAND

ISBN 0-373-17301-6

LOVE LIKE GOLD

First North American Publication 1996.

Copyright © 1992 by Valerie Parv.

Printed in U.S.A.

PROLOGUE

HE HAD to have her.

A gleam like a flame flared in Tom Callander's arctic blue eyes as he stared at the screen. Lifting his head, he spoke over his shoulder. 'Hold it right there, Ned.'

The picture froze on a giant close-up of the woman's face, and Tom leaned forward, resting his forearms on his knees as he studied her. Woman? She had been a child when this was made, seventeen or eighteen at the most. Or else the dewy-eyed innocence she projected so powerfully was entirely faked, in which case she was one hell of an actress.

Never taking his eyes from the screen, he studied her feature by feature. With wide-set almond eyes almost too large for her heart-shaped face, she wasn't conventionally beautiful. Her mouth was too strong, for one thing, hinting at a determination which wasn't part of the character she was playing. But she had an allure that went beyond beauty. It made him want to lift her down off the screen and make love to her until she was dizzy.

He straightened, surprised at his own reactions. He had assessed hundreds of actresses in his career, and none of them had affected him so personally. He almost laughed aloud. It proved one of two things: either she was perfect for the part of Katie Dooley, or she was perfect for him, which meant he should watch himself. Knowing who she was, Tom didn't need the aggravation.

He snapped his fingers and the picture moved on, showing her in a long-shot which emphasised her delicate build. She was about five foot five, Tom guessed, with a waist he could span with two hands, although her breasts contradicted her small stature—they were far too womanly for a seventeen-year-old. He licked suddenly dry lips. She was the darnedest mix of saint and sinner he'd ever seen on a screen.

He tried to imagine her now, seven or eight years on. The innocence would be gone. No woman with her looks could survive to her mid-twenties without learning something about love and life.

A stab of pain made him glance at his hands in surprise. Picturing her with a lover, he'd ground his nails into his palms. As if he cared what she did or with whom! She might look innocent, but after what she'd done to his family he wasn't fooled. Now that it was time to settle the score, he was surprised to find that she was so talented. It made his plan almost ridiculously easy.

'Do you want to see the second reel?' Ned queried through the intercom that connected Tom with the projection booth behind him.

He took a last lingering look at the screen. 'No, you can stop it there. I've seen all I need to.'

The film faded from the screen and he blinked as the house lights came up.

Ned emerged from his cubbyhole. 'I told you it was a waste of time. The word is, it was too bad for commercial release.' He looked hard at Tom, seeing something unexpected in his expression, and groaned. 'Don't tell me you *liked* it?'

Tom shook his head and massaged the dark highlights at his temples with stiff fingers. 'Not the film—the girl who played the *ingénue*. She's riveting.'

'Now I understand why you wanted to sit through this thing. But you're wasting your time. She's out of the business, and word is nothing will get her in front of a camera again.'

Tom's eyes gleamed and his jaw firmed in a gesture Ned had learned to read well. He began to feel sorry for the young woman, knowing how persistent Tom Callander could be when his mind was made up. Instinct told Ned it was made up now.

He wasn't wrong. 'It's a sin to waste such talent,' Tom swore. 'You saw her yourself. She lights up the screen without trying.'

Ned's palms lifted in a defensive gesture. 'Easy, boss, don't shoot the messenger. I didn't say she isn't talented, only that she isn't available at any price.'

Tom uncoiled from the cinema seat, his six foot one in height dwarfing the small room. If he hadn't been one of Australia's best directors—or the world's, for that matter, since he had made as many films in Hollywood as he had in his home country—he could have been a force in the acting world. His burnished gold hair with the trademark dark highlights at his temples was the sort women liked to run their fingers through. Dark brows framed compellingly blue eyes shot with yellow through the iris. They could transfix a difficult player with terror, or coax a nervous actor into an Oscar-winning performance.

Trimly proportioned, with a generous mouth, he had one flaw—a tracery of fine scars along his jawline, courtesy of a teenage sporting accident. The scars were hardly noticeable most of the time but turned white when he was angry, like a beacon, warning others to keep their distance.

The scars were invisible now because Tom wasn't angry, but his mouth was set in an implacable line and his eyes blazed with a determination Ned hadn't seen in a long time. 'What are you going to do?' he asked warily.

Tom's wry smile barely lessened his purposeful look. 'What do you think? My Katie Dooley is out there, and I intend to have her.'

CHAPTER ONE

ANNE FLEMING pushed the hair back from her eyes and lifted her face to the welcome breeze from the air-conditioner. 'We must be heading for a storm,' she told Nancy, the secretary, who greeted her in the cramped reception area. 'The temperature's climbed eleven degrees in the last hour.'

'It was over thirty when the kids woke me up this morning,' the other woman agreed. 'Still, that's Kalgoorlie for you.'

Anne sighed. 'Why can't gold be found somewhere nice and temperate instead of in a country fit for nobody but sheep and rabbits?'

Nancy laughed. 'At least you chose your profession. I made the mistake of marrying a geologist. Nobody warned me what I was letting myself in for!'

Anne frequently worked in the field with Nancy's husband and occasionally babysat their two children, so she knew Nancy's complaints were mostly for show. 'You wouldn't swap Greg for all the businessmen in Perth—admit it.'

Before Nancy could answer, the inner door opened and Anne's boss, Sam O'Neill, peered out. 'Ah, Anne, you're here.'

'I was told you wanted to see me urgently,' she said, curiosity colouring her voice as she followed Sam into his office.

He settled his rotund frame on a corner of his desk, letting one leg swing free. At fifty-two, he was the exploration manager of Waterford Mining, and the nearest to a father figure Anne had. She loved him and respected him, both as a person and a fellow scientist.

Knowing how he liked to keep her in suspense when a new assignment was pending, she kept silent, refusing to give him the satisfaction of knowing how curious she was.

When she could stand it no longer, she said, 'Don't tell me, the owners of the Last Resort mine have agreed to our joint venture proposition?' She had come across the mine during work in another area, and started negotiations to involve the company. Proven mining reserves were already defined, but the owners were being difficult. If she had pulled it off, it would be a real feather in her cap.

'No, it isn't the Last Resort—I only wish it were,' said Sam, dashing her hopes. 'It's a new project altogether, what you might call a public relations exercise.'

Her heart sank. 'Oh, Sam, you know how I feel about being the token woman geo. Just because there are only a handful of us working in the field, it's no excuse to thrust us into the public eye at every opportunity.'

'I don't think of you as a token anything,' he said. 'I chose you for this assignment because you're the best we have and you know the country beyond Leonora to the Terraces better than anyone else.'

A frown furrowed her brow. 'The Terraces? But we have no mining interests up that way. For one thing, it's too far north to cart ore to our mill, although I suppose we can build another mill if there's a big enough gold deposit.'

'This doesn't involve grass-roots prospecting. I want you to guide someone through the area.'

'Since when did we go into the tourism business?'

Sam patted his few strands of hair into place self-consciously. 'The man you're to guide isn't a tourist. He's a film director who needs help scouting locations for his next picture.'

The bottom dropped out of Anne's stomach. 'Film director? Oh, no, Sam, this isn't my line of work at all. Couldn't you get one of the other geos, or the field foreman?'

'The other geologists are either in the field or on R and R. You're it, I'm afraid.' He tapped his foot. 'Actually, I'm surprised you're so resistant to the idea. I thought you'd enjoy the change of pace.'

He seemed to expect some sort of explanation for her attitude. Anne dropped long, sooty lashes over her hazel eyes, which were suddenly brighter than she wanted him to see.

She was relieved when the telephone rang and he picked it up, listened for a moment, then covered the mouthpiece and stage-whispered, 'Sorry, but it's the hospital.'

Anne knew that Sam's elderly mother was in hospital in Perth, having surgery on an arthritic hip, so she nodded and moved discreetly across the office, helping herself to coffee from the dripolator.

Staring out of the window, she sipped the coffee and tried to marshal her whirling thoughts. Sam was obviously disappointed by her lack of enthusiasm for the new assignment. What would he say if he knew that it was because she had grown up around film people and few of her memories were pleasant ones?

She glanced at Sam, but he was still engrossed in his phone call. He was a good friend and she had never lied to him. She had simply never corrected his assumption that her mother was retired. How would he react to the discovery that her mother was Joanna Flame, the actress hailed by the critics as the Australian Elizabeth Taylor?

Being known as Joanna Flame's daughter hadn't bothered Anne until her teens. Even the mother-and-daughter outfits and lookalike hairstyles Joanna preferred hadn't troubled her unduly. Anne—Deanne, as she was known then—had assumed that all mother-daughter relationships were the same.

It wasn't until Joanna arranged her first audition that everything had changed. A shudder gripped Anne as the memory forced its way to the surface, refusing to be blotted out even now.

At sixteen she had looked older, thanks to Joanna's ministrations. She pictured herself tottering into the director's office on absurdly high heels, feeling like a clown in her mother's make-up.

Ushering her to a couch instead of one of the chairs, the director had settled himself beside her, opening a script across both their knees, which were practically touching. At first, she had believed his touch under the pages was accidental. When it happened again, fear had shrilled through her. When she tried to move away he forced her back on to the couch, covering her painted lips and smothering her cries with his mouth.

Luckily they were interrupted by an assistant investigating her cries, and Anne had darted out of the office, leaving the director spluttering futilely behind her.

Shaken and dishevelled, she had rushed to the studio cafeteria where her mother waited. When she stammered out her story, her mother had put an arm around her shoulders. 'Poor baby! I should have gone with you. Next time I will, I promise.'

Anne recalled staring at her mother in bewilderment. 'Next time? What about this time? Aren't you going to do anything about that horrible man?'

She would never forget her mother's wistful expression. 'There's nothing I *can* do, darling. I need these people—*we* need them, to survive. When you're older, you'll understand, my pet. I'm only sorry you had to find out so early about how this industry works.'

At that moment Anne had felt something wither inside her. If only her beloved father hadn't died in that senseless car accident when she was ten. He would have put things right, she was sure, instead of telling her it was the way things were.

If that was how the industry worked, she wanted no part of it, she had resolved. She had kept her vow, breaking it to make one film at her mother's insistence, and then only because she needed money to pay her university fees and gain her science degree. Joanna had refused to help unless she made the film.

Fortunately, the film was never commercially released, and Anne had used her degree to carve out a career as a gold geologist, first in North Queensland, then with Waterford Mining in Kalgoorlie, putting as much distance between herself and her mother's world as she could.

Why couldn't the past leave her alone? She'd thought herself safe from recognition in the harsh conditions of the outback mining community. Everyone here came from somewhere else, and they all had their own reasons for staying. All that mattered was how well you did your job and supported the other members of the team. Unless you chose to reveal it, the past was your own affair.

Until now, she thought unhappily. Now she had to convince Sam that she couldn't guide his film director through the outback, without destroying the anonymity she had carefully nurtured.

She heard Sam replace the receiver and swung around. 'How's your mother?' she asked.

'Better than a woman in her seventies has any right to be, according to her doctor,' he said with a relieved smile. Knowing how close he was to his mother, Anne returned his smile gladly. He had been looking so haunted lately that she was sure his mother's illness must be the reason.

But he had another problem, which surprised her. 'I can see you intend to turn down this assignment,' he said. 'But, before you do, there's something you should know. Things aren't as good at Waterford as they could be. Money's tight, and involvement in a prestige film would benefit us enormously. The producers are willing to pay well for our technical advice and the use of our locations.'

Her eyes were wide with shock. 'Why didn't you tell me things were difficult?'

'I haven't told anyone, and I'd appreciate you keeping it in confidence. But you can see why I'm keen to co-operate with the film people?'

Anne felt as if the breath had been punched out of her. How could she turn Sam down now? Yet the idea of taking on the assignment filled her with revulsion.

He saw how conflicted she was. 'You needn't decide right away,' he relented. 'Why don't you meet the director and talk the project over with him before you make up your mind?'

As reprieves went, it wasn't much, but it saved her from having to answer right away. She had never dreamed she would be faced with such a dilemma here, of all places. She needed time to come to terms with Sam's request. 'All right,' she conceded. 'Who's the director, and when do I meet him?'

Sam's relief was almost palpable. 'Good girl, I knew you wouldn't let me down. His name is Thomas Callander, and he's waiting in your office right now.'

At the sound of the name, her knees went weak and coffee sloshed around in her cup. It couldn't be, could it? 'Now?' she echoed bleakly. 'But...'

'I checked your schedule. You're free for the rest of the day, so it's the ideal time.'

'But I have a mountain of paperwork to catch up on.'

He swept aside her objection. 'I'll have Nancy clear some of the backlog for you.' He stood up.

'Don't look so worried. Tom Callander doesn't bite. He's only a film director.'

Only anything didn't apply to the man waiting for her in her office. He rose as she and Sam walked in, and Anne was immediately dwarfed by his towering height. No, not just by his height, she admitted, but by his presence. He was the kind of man who drew all eyes the moment he walked into a room.

'Anne Fleming, Thomas Callander,' Sam performed the introductions.

She offered her hand. 'How do you do, Mr Callander?'

'Tom, please.' Her small hand was immediately enveloped in a grip which would have been crushing if not for the restraint she felt him exercising. Mr Callander obviously took good care of his body, which, to her trained observer's eye, was magnificent.

'I understand you want to make a film in this area, Mr . . . Tom,' she said with an effort. Nothing had prepared her for the man's amazing impact on her senses, and she wondered what was the matter with her.

She worked with men all the time, most of them athletic types whose work demanded a degree of physical fitness. Even seeing them wander around a mining camp half clothed had never reduced her to this state, as if every nerve-ending was on fire. She felt raw and vulnerable, more aware than ever that she was a woman in a man's world.

To her chagrin, Tom Callander seemed aware of it too. 'When Sam told me he'd find me someone to help scout locations, I never realised it would be someone so bewitching,' he told her.

Sam sensed her annoyance at the blatantly sexist remark. 'Anne is one of our senior geologists, with vast experience at exploring and mapping the areas you want to visit.'

Tom's heavy-lidded gaze stayed on her until she grew warm under his scrutiny. 'Brains as well as beauty—I'm really in luck,' he said languidly.

He seemed to be waiting for her to say something. It was almost as if he was deliberately goading her with his comments, testing her to see if she would respond.

She had the uncomfortable feeling that he wanted more from her than help finding film locations. But what? He couldn't know who she was. Her appearance was totally changed from the days when she'd lived with her mother. She had allowed her hair to return to its natural dark chestnut and rarely wore make-up any more, other than for special occasions. Her khaki drill shirt and trousers were hardly glamorous.

Satisfied that nothing about her could remind him of her past, she forced a smile. 'I'm glad you find me satisfactory, Mr Callander. But I haven't yet agreed to take this assignment, only to talk it over with you.' There, let him think he had already blown his chance with his sexist remarks.

His gaze shifted to Sam and one dark eyebrow lifted speculatively. 'I understood the decision was made, Sam.'

Sam looked uncomfortable. Evidently he hadn't been prepared for the depth of Anne's opposition either, and had given Tom Callander the impression that it was all settled. 'This job is outside contract requirements, so the decision is up to Anne,' he said reluctantly.

A fleeting look of annoyance crossed Tom's face, but was instantly masked. 'I see. And do I pass muster, Miss Fleming?'

'It's the job which has to pass muster,' she echoed, unable to suppress her irritation. Why was he behaving as if they had to like each other? Surely it was enough to find the locations he wanted? What he thought of her as a person couldn't possibly matter.

His wide mouth relaxed into an ironic smile. 'Quite so. Which is why I asked Sam to arrange this lunch, so I can fill you in on what I want to do here.'

Going to lunch with him had no part in her plans. How could Sam do this to her? Anne shot him a look of appeal, but his eyes were fixed on his hands, as if he knew what she was thinking.

She felt a flash of sympathy for the cattle she had seen herded into ever-narrower races until they were finally corralled and branded. In spite of herself, she felt an infuriating flicker of excitement, as if some small part of her *wanted* to be corralled by Tom Callander. The idea was abhorrent, and yet it persisted until she asked Sam, 'Have you scheduled anything else I ought to know about?'

He shook his head. 'No, just lunch.' He glanced at his watch. 'I must get back to the office. You two enjoy your meeting, won't you?'

She wouldn't, she was sure. Mr Tom Callander was much too self-possessed for her to feel comfortable around him. She had the uncanny feeling that there was more to him than his sexist remarks and provocative behaviour suggested. He didn't look like a man who needed to resort to clichéd comments to interest a woman. So why was he acting this way with her?

He had asked her a question and was waiting for a reply, she realised. 'I'm sorry, I wasn't paying attention,' she apologised.

'I said, since this is your domain, I'll defer to your choice of lunch venue,' he repeated with exaggerated patience.

Again, she felt that fish-on-a-line feeling, as if he was playing with her. She shook herself inwardly, annoyed with herself for being unusually fanciful. It was more her mother's trait than hers, normally. 'I have no preferences,' she said. 'Most of us eat in the company dining-room when we're working in town, or I cook myself a scratch meal at home.'

'In that case, I passed a small French place on the way here. It looks new. Would you like to go there?'

She knew the restaurant he meant. 'It opened a couple of weeks ago, so I haven't tried it, although it looks nice,' she said noncommittally.

'Chez François it is, then.'

She looked down at her clothes. 'I'm not really dressed for restaurant dining,' she prevaricated.

His warm gaze roved over the curves her working clothes did little to conceal, ending at the shadow between her full breasts where the top button had come undone. She resisted the urge to fasten it. If they were to work together, she would have to stop reacting so sensitively. *If* they worked together, she added mentally. If there was a way to avoid it, she still intended to take it.

'From what I saw, the standard looked reasonably casual,' he said. 'But if you'd be more comfortable somewhere else, we can go there.'

'No, your choice is fine,' she said with an impatient sigh. All she wanted was for this to be over so she could get back to the work she loved. Her very response to Tom Callander had reminded her vividly of all the reasons why she wanted nothing to do with his world.

He was right about the restaurant. It was a cheery place with red and white chequered cloths covering dark timber tables. At the back, a small glassed-in courtyard protected diners from the heat outside, while preserving the feeling of dining al fresco. Large baskets of dark green ferns hung from rafters overhead, adding to the outdoor feeling.

Anne barely noticed the surroundings, being too intent on the man who took his seat opposite her at a quiet corner table. How could fate have been so unkind as to have brought him to her? He didn't seem to share her tension.

'I didn't expect French cuisine in an outback mining town,' he commented.

'Kalgoorlie is the largest urban centre outside Perth,' she pointed out. 'We have something like ten banks, thirty or so hotels and a population of about thirty thousand.'

The mild reproof drew his dark eyebrows upwards. 'I stand corrected. Obviously, Sam O'Neill put me in touch with an authority on the area.'

Mentally Anne cursed herself for showing off. She had intended to convince him that she wasn't the right person to guide him around the area, but her first words had done just the opposite. 'It's all in the tourist brochures,' she said lightly. 'I'm no expert on the gold country.'

His gaze intensified and the fingers playing with the cutlery tightened visibly. 'Sam says you are. According to him, you've made a study of the ghost towns of the eastern goldfields, over and above your work as a geologist.'

'Sam exaggerates,' she said through clenched teeth. 'It's a hobby, that's all.'

'But you do know your way around the country north of Menzies to the Terraces, which is the area where I want to film.'

Her dismay was ill-disguised. 'That's some of the most hostile country anywhere. A lot of it's deep sand, mountainous wash-outs and sump-killing tree roots. Going in on foot is tough enough, without a film crew in tow.'

There was amusement in his mild gaze. 'You sound as if you don't think I'm up to it.'

'I've no doubt you can handle anything,' she said coolly, determined not to be drawn into an analysis of his masculine virtues. 'It's your crew and film equipment I'm concerned about.'

Interest flickered in his blue eyes. 'You seem to know something of what's involved.'

Alarm bells sounded in her head. 'We've had other film crews out here,' she improvised. She was saved from further probing by the arrival of their first course, a cocktail of lobster tails flown in from the coast.

Tom ate with relish, giving the dish his single-minded attention, as she had a feeling he did most things. Only when the last morsel was gone did he restart their discussion. 'Did Sam tell you what my film is about?' he asked.

'He left it to you, but he mentioned it's a prestige film, so I gather it's a large-scale production.'

'The largest,' he confirmed. 'I want it to be absolutely authentic, as a flagship for the new studio complex I'm building north of Perth.'

The intensity of his voice made her look up. 'This project sounds important to you,' she remarked.

'It is. Apart from being the biggest film ever made in Australia, it will establish Callander Studios as a force in film production around the globe.'

'But you already have a world-wide reputation,' she said in surprise.

He nodded, accepting the compliment for the fact that it was. 'Granted, but there are greater pinnacles to conquer. I have films up here,' he tapped his tanned forehead, 'that can only be made on a grand scale, by a studio under my absolute control.'

Coming from another man, the plan might have sounded grandiose, but Tom Callander made success seem inevitable. In spite of herself, Anne was impressed. 'I hope you succeed,' she said in all sincerity.

Like a steel trap, his hand sprang across the table and closed on her wrist. 'Then help me *make* it succeed,' he urged. '*Kalgoorlie Gold* is the picture to do it, if you help me.'

Twisting free of his grasp was impossible. There was too much strength in the steel circle of his fingers, so she kept her hand still. It was less easy to control the pulses of electrical sensation which radiated along her arm from the contact.

'I don't see how I can make a difference,' she dissembled, hating the tremor in her voice which betrayed her inner turmoil.

'You can provide the technical expertise and the historical know-how I need.' Tom finally realised he was still holding her wrist and released it, then sat back, his eyes ablaze. '*Kalgoorlie Gold* will be the Australian *Gone with the Wind*.

'Think of it, Anne, a sweeping saga of romance and drama taking in all the grandeur of the Gold Rush. You know that Herbert Hoover worked out here before becoming President of the United States of America?'

'He managed the Sons of Gwalia mine at the turn of the century,' she supplied.

'He's to be a key figure in my film, along with another colourful historical figure, the Aboriginal bandit, Coyle.'

'You've certainly done your homework,' she agreed. 'There's plenty of rich material there. But where does the romance come in?'

He leaned forward, resuming his drumming with the cutlery as if his restless energy was too much to contain. 'History has its limitations, so I created a fictional assistant to Mr Hoover, who falls in love with a local schoolteacher. Eventually they help Coyle to escape from a white prison and return to his own people.'

Her lips pursed in a soundless whistle. 'I see what you mean about an Australian *Gone with the Wind*!'

'Then you'll help me to make it possible?'

Anne was saved from replying when the waitress served their main course of chicken breasts baked in clay. The chestnut sauce teased at her nostrils when the clay was broken to reveal the meat. Tom barely concealed his impatience while their vegetables were served. As soon as they were alone again, he repeated his question.

Her appetite was instantly quenched by the answer she knew she had to give. 'I'm sorry, but I can't,' she told him.

'You can't or you won't?'

'Both, I suppose. Sam made it my decision, and I'd rather not be involved. I'm sorry if you've wasted a lunch on me.'

The gaze he turned on her was bleak, as if she had forced him into a corner. 'It isn't wasted, Anne,' he said in a low voice that sent shivers of warning down her spine as he added, 'Or should I say *Deanne*?'

Her horrified expression met his hard gaze as her fork clattered against her plate. 'You know about me.' It wasn't a question. If he knew her real name, there was very little else he didn't know.

'I know.'

'Then why this charade?'

'It isn't a charade,' he assured her. 'My request is genuine.'

A heavy weight settled around her heart. 'What if I don't agree to help you?'

His cold gaze pierced her to her core. 'We both know the answer to that.'

'You'll tell everyone who I am,' she said in a thin, defeated voice.

'It's not my problem if you're ashamed of who you are,' he said harshly.

Anne's head jerked back. 'I happen to like my privacy, but it doesn't mean I'm ashamed of my background.'

He tilted a questioning eyebrow. 'Nor of anything done in your name?'

'What's that supposed to mean?' she demanded.

'I'm sure you can work it out. You may have thought you could hide here forever, but you must have known your past would catch up with you sooner or later?'

The way he said 'your past' made it sound as if she had done something terrible, when her only crime was to want to live her life her own way. What was so wrong with that?

'Then you'll do it?' he persisted when she kept silent.

What choice did she have? 'Yes, but not willingly. You're even more cold-blooded and manipulative than the people I came here to avoid.'

He raised his glass. 'Coming from someone like you, that's practically a compliment.'

Once, just once, Anne wished she possessed some of her mother's outrageousness. It would have been so satisfying to snatch up her wine glass and fling the contents into his handsome, devilish face.

CHAPTER TWO

NANCY perched on the edge of Anne's bed and cupped her hands around her coffee-mug, watching her pack with wide, excited eyes. 'Lucky you, getting to work with a film producer.'

Anne's fingers plucked at the shirt she was meant to be folding. 'It's hardly luck when I wasn't given a choice,' she shrugged.

Nancy raised a questioning eyebrow. 'You mean you'd actually turn down the chance to work with that gorgeous man I saw coming out of your office last week?'

Remembering how Nancy had contrived to pass her office just as Tom Callander emerged, Anne smiled, then grew serious. 'Honestly, Nance, appearances aren't everything.'

'Then you do admit he's gorgeous?'

'He's all right, I suppose.' Not for anything would Anne admit to her friend how Tom had haunted her for the last week, as she prepared for this expedition.

Although she had tried to dismiss him from her mind, his commanding presence had dominated her thoughts. She had only to drop her guard for a moment and he was back, taunting her with that clear blue gaze, so knowing and aware, as if he knew the secrets of her soul. Which was nonsense, of course. He might know she was Joanna Flame's daughter, but that was all. The rest was the result of her overworked imagination, which she would do well to curb before she saw him again.

'It will do you good to spend some time with a real live hunk for once, instead of wandering around the outback with only your compass for companionship,' Nancy said with mock severity. 'Sometimes I swear you forget you're female.'

It was a familiar lament, and Anne resisted the urge to sigh deeply. 'If I am left on the shelf, it won't be your fault.' Most of her friend's gatherings included an eligible male whom Anne 'just had to meet'.

Between the workaholic, the hopeless male chauvinist and the practical joker she had met so far through Nancy, Anne couldn't decide which man she disliked most. Since men outnumbered eligible women in the goldfields, they had all wanted to see her again, but she had turned them down as politely as she could.

'You could at least have given that nice Peter Andreas a chance,' Nancy said.

He was the workaholic, Anne recalled, searching her memory. 'I did, twice. He broke one date to fly to Perth on business, and the second date turned out to be a mapping trip—hardly a romantic liaison. Face it, Nancy, I'm better off as I am, doing the job of my choice and living as I please.'

'And working off your maternal instincts on the local kids,' Nancy murmured.

Anne turned aside to disguise the brightness that glittered in her eyes. It was a sore point between them that Anne resisted male entanglements yet gave her free time unstintingly to the young people in the area.

Most mining towns had a problem providing enough activities to keep teenagers occupied. Those who weren't affiliated with sporting groups often found themselves at a loose end and chanced getting into trouble. So many of their parents were transient workers that the youngsters seldom had time to develop their own social circle.

Having experienced some of their problems herself, Anne identified with the youngsters more than Nancy ever suspected. Currently, both women served on a fund-raising committee to establish a new drop-in centre where young people could enjoy themselves and prepare to join the workforce.

'I didn't say I'll never marry, and you know I want children some day, but I'll wait until the right man comes along,' she said, ending the discussion. The telephone rang and she answered it, glad of the diversion. 'Hello?'

'Good, you're home.' Her hand tightened involuntarily around the receiver as she recognised Tom Callander's husky tones. 'I need to see you about a few final details. Is it OK if I come over? Sam gave me your address.'

Her gaze jumped around the room. As a single person, she only qualified for bed-sitter accommodation, although she had been shopping around for something more spacious to rent privately. Now she was immediately conscious of the bed which dominated her small quarters, and every nerve rejected the idea of Tom visiting her here. 'No, I—er—I have to go out. I'll come and see you. Where are you staying?'

'As you wish.' Amusement tinged his tone as he gave her the name of his hotel, which was new and predictably luxurious. 'What time will you be here?'

It was already early afternoon. If she preserved the fiction that she was indeed going out, it would be late by the time she reached his suite. She cursed herself for the lie, as she named a time.

'Fine. We could be here a while, so I'll have some food sent in. Is there anything you particularly don't like?'

Film people, she was tempted to say, but held her tongue. Baiting him might tempt him to unmask her as Joanna Flame's daughter, destroying her precious anonymity. It was better to be civil. He couldn't stay forever, after all. 'No, there's nothing I don't like,' she admitted wearily.

She saw Nancy's interested glance and knew she would have some explaining to do when she hung up. But all Tom Callander said was, 'I'll see you later.'

Having said she was going out, Anne was con-science-driven to invent an errand. She decided to drive the few miles out of town to visit the tem-porary home of the youth centre. Driving along the broad expanse of Hannan Street, which was as wide as a six-lane highway, a legacy of the days when it was used to turn camel trains around during the Gold Rush, she let her thoughts drift.

Clearing her desk and preparing to work with Tom Callander had left little time for thinking. Now there was no avoiding it. She scowled and her knuckles tightened around the steering-wheel.

If only she could turn the clock back a few days. She would be planning her next field visit. Most of the preliminary work had already been done. Now someone else had taken over the, to Anne, more exciting stage of studying the old workings and taking mineral samples to determine the gold-bearing prospects.

Instead she was stuck with guiding Tom Callander around the goldfields, knowing that each step they took could bring her nearer to disaster. If he found the locations he was looking for, his film crew would soon follow.

Anne shuddered, remembering only too well the circus which was involved. It wasn't just a few cameramen and actors. There would be make-up people, catering crews, costume hands, gaffers with their miles of electrical gadgets, and an army of clerical people to keep it all straight.

She blinked as salty tears crowded her eyes. If she was honest, it wasn't the people she really minded. It was the inevitability of someone from the past recognising her.

It wasn't fair! She had made a wonderful life for herself away from all that. In the goldfields, she was plain Anne Fleming, not the pretentious 'Deanne' which she'd always hated. She stood or fell on her own merits, and so far she'd stood pretty well.

Now everything was bound to change. The thought that Nancy might stop pairing her with awful men and treat her with the same awe she did Tom Callander filled Anne with dismay. Was it wrong to want things to stay the same? She was happy as she was. She wanted nothing to do with her mother's shallow, frivolous world.

'It will do you good to spend time with a real live hunk for once. Sometimes...you forget you're female.'

Nancy's words nagged at her. She hadn't forgotten, had she? Her glossy, shoulder-length hair was carefully styled. Her nails were cared for and her clothes...well, they could use some updating, she acknowledged ruefully. Spending so much time out in the field, she had little use for dressing up.

'Damn!' She slammed her hands down on the steering-wheel, the force jarring all the way to her elbows. Until Tom Callander arrived, she had been perfectly happy with her appearance. Taking stock of herself reminded her of her mother when a juicy part was on offer. Well, she was damned if she would do the same, not for Tom Callander or any man like him.

It was just as well she'd chosen to visit the drop-in centre. By the time she'd discussed future fund-raising plans with the co-ordinator, she felt more composed and some of the hectic colour had left her cheeks.

After a cup of tea and a chat with some of the young people who were helping to decorate the temporary centre, she had banished most of her fears. This was the reality, not Tom Callander's cardboard cut-out world.

The receptionist at his hotel raised a speculative eyebrow when Anne asked for Tom's room number and insisted on letting him know that Anne was on her way up. Goodness knew what the gossips would make of it, she thought crossly as the elevator rose with agonising slowness to the penthouse floor.

Tom obviously couldn't care less about gossip, because he opened the door dressed in an Oriental-style silk robe which only reached his thighs. In spite of her resolve, Anne's eyes were drawn to the triangle of dark chest hair revealed above the tie belt. Droplets of moisture beaded the curls and slicked his head. She must have interrupted his shower.

'Am I too early?' she asked through lips gone suddenly dry, a reaction caused by pure dislike, she told herself.

His gesture ushered her into a spacious living area beyond which she glimpsed a bedroom and bathroom. 'No, come in and make yourself comfortable. I'll only be a moment, then we can talk.'

She had assumed he meant to change, but he strode to a telephone and picked up the receiver which lay beside it, continuing the call which her arrival had interrupted.

When he finished, he dropped on to the sofa opposite her and rested one muscular arm along the back of it. 'Now we can get down to business,' he said.

Anne swallowed around a huge lump in her throat. 'Don't you want to change first?'

His arctic gaze flickered over her choice of white silk oversized shirt belted over slim-fitting cream trousers. There was nothing the least bit provocative about the outfit, but somehow he managed to make her feel under-dressed.

She resisted the urge to clutch at the open neck of her shirt as alarm shrilled through her. What had he expected? Oh, lord, was this meeting a euphemism for something else? Was it starting already?

But he uncoiled from the sofa with the grace of a panther and looked down at her, his eyes glittering, but whether with anger or amusement, she couldn't tell. 'I'll humour you for now,' he said drily. 'But remember, I know who you are, so the act is wasted on me.'

Her hair spun in a soft cloud around her head as she shook it violently. 'I don't understand. This isn't any act.'

'Oh, no? Then the brazen little madam I remember must have been the act. Right down to the skimpy black off-the-shoulder dress and tons of make-up.'

Anne hunched into herself, crossing her arms defensively over her chest. 'I didn't think you remembered.'

'You mean you hoped I didn't.'

It was true. As soon as she heard his name, the memory had come rushing back, but when he'd said nothing she had convinced herself that he'd forgotten their first meeting.

She had been visiting the set of her mother's latest film, which she did rarely because she hated Joanna's condescending behaviour towards the people she worked with. Anne saw film-making as a team effort, but Joanna insisted that remaining aloof enhanced her star status.

Too shy to argue, Anne had gone along, but stayed in the background as much as possible while they were introduced to the crew. It wasn't difficult, as all eyes were on Joanna, except for one sapphire pair which raked her from top to toe. She had waited until the others moved on before asking the young producer, 'Why are you staring at me?'

His gravel laugh was humourless. 'I'm surprised you have to ask, in a dress like that. Or should I call it a man-trap?'

The dress was her mother's choice and made Anne feel hideously uncomfortable, but this arrogant man had no right to judge her, all the same. 'I don't recall asking for your opinion,' she said, trying to imitate Joanna's queenly behaviour.

Nevertheless, his look of disgust stung her, although no more than his derisive comment, 'My, my, the cub has claws just like her mother. What a pair you make—one as bad as the other.'

He had walked away, leaving her no right of reply. She felt cheap and longed to tell him that she wasn't the kind of person he thought. Why his opinion should matter so much, she wasn't sure. She only knew that it did. But she hadn't seen the young producer again, until now.

His opinion of her hadn't improved, she gathered from his cold expression. He was still as arrogant and judgemental as ever, when he didn't know the first thing about her. 'Who made you the judge and jury of my morals anyway?' she asked, her voice shaky but defiant.

He seemed utterly unmoved by her anger. 'I'm self-appointed. Anyone who flaunts herself the way you do and carries on as if no one else in the world matters deserves all she gets.'

'You're talking about the past. It has nothing to do with the present,' she said stiffly.

'Ah, yes, the past. Which brings me to my next question. Why did you decide to bury yourself out here for so long, Deanne?'

'What I do with my life is no concern of yours—and my name is Anne,' she said through clenched teeth.

'But you don't deny that you're running away? Could your conscience be troubling you, by any chance?'

He was crazy. 'Why should it?' she tossed at him. In the beginning, her mother had been hurt by her choice of career, but even Joanna had mellowed gradually, realising the advantages of *not* having a grown daughter around to remind everyone that she was growing older. 'I've done nothing I'm ashamed of,' she added as he continued to regard her with thinly veiled contempt.

'No regrets at all?' he asked.

If he meant about abandoning her old way of life, there was only one possible answer, and her chin lifted defiantly as she gave it. 'Not a one.'

Gold sparks flared in his blue eyes and she looked away from their brilliance, focusing instead on a tracery of scars along his jawline. They gleamed whitely against his tanned skin and she felt a sudden urge to trace them with her finger. She jammed her hands into her pockets to still the impulse.

'No matter what you call yourself, you're still the same Deanne Flame,' he ground out. 'Only the packaging has changed.'

Anne jumped to her feet. 'Then I'm surprised you want to trouble yourself with me. I'm sure if I explain the situation Sam will find another geo to guide you around the goldfields.'

'I don't want another geologist, I want you.'

She blinked to dispel a sudden gathering of tears. 'Why? Is it to satisfy some petty urge for revenge because I offended you years ago?'

His mocking smile didn't quite reach those compelling eyes. 'I've been called many things, Miss Fleming, but petty isn't among them.'

Anne twisted her hands together. 'Then why do you want me?

'If, as you say, your conscience is clear, then my reasons shouldn't matter to you. What does matter is that I get this film off and running in time for the opening of my new studio complex. For that, I need the best people around me, and Sam assures me you qualify.'

Why did Sam have to champion her to Tom Callander, of all people? Normally she would have been flattered, but this time she wished Sam had been more restrained. She could never convince Tom to recruit someone else now.

Her sigh of resignation was a soft breeze between them. 'In that case, let's get this over with.'

'No.' His sharp denial startled her. 'Your half-hearted co-operation isn't good enough. I'm paying Sam top dollar to get top results. I want your assurance that I'll get my money's worth.'

The pulse at her throat throbbed with the intensity of her dislike for this man who thought he could buy anything he wanted, even people. It was so typical of his kind. 'Or you'll do what, cancel the deal?' she asked, annoyed as her voice betrayed her with its huskiness.

'I'll do worse than that,' he said. There was no mistaking the seriousness of his threat. 'I'll start by calling the local papers, then my contacts in national television and anyone else I can think of. They'll be fascinated by the life Joanna Flame's daughter has been living.'

Weakness swept through her. She had not the slightest doubt that he would do what he said. By the time he finished, there wouldn't be a town in Australia where she could hide her true identity. 'I can't believe you'd be so despicable,' she cried.

'Believe it,' he assured her. 'You may as well know now that I play to win. It's up to you which side you're on.'

'Do I have a choice?'

'None whatsoever, that I can see.'

Conflicting emotions warred within her. Giving in would help the company and protect her secret. Anything else was unthinkable—and yet instinct warned her that Tom wouldn't respect her if she gave in too readily. It was crazy, but she found herself wanting his respect very much. 'I'll co-operate on one condition,' she said, striving to keep her voice level.

He angled his hip against a side-table and folded his arms across his chest, exposing a wider expanse of dark, hair-strewn body. The sight played havoc with her senses until it was an effort to remain clear-headed as she knew she must. 'You're hardly in a position to set conditions,' he warned her. 'But I'm willing to listen.'

'I want your word that if I do what you ask you won't reveal my family background to anyone.'

'I'm not the only person in Australia who can put two and two together,' he reminded her.

'But you are the only one who's tracked me down so far. I'd still like to know how you managed it.' *And why*, she added to herself.

'I didn't find out you were here until after I decided to film in the goldfields,' he admitted. 'My clipping service sent me all the background they could lay their hands on.'

'The photo in the local paper,' she said on a heavy outrush of breath. As a member of the fund-raising committee for the new youth centre, she'd been photographed with the others, although she'd tried to avoid it. She could hardly credit that it had led Tom to her, but what other explanation was there?

'Your picture was familiar, yet the name meant nothing to me until I came across an earlier photo of you and made the connection,' he explained.

It was as if fate had led him to her. 'Do I have your promise not to tell anyone else?' she asked, refusing to be sidetracked.

There was a tension-laden pause as he regarded her from under hooded lids. She kept her gaze steady, waiting for his answer. 'I can't promise,' he said at last.

As she opened her mouth to protest, he made a slashing gesture. 'I can give you my word not to reveal your identity until my crew gets here. After that, there's too much chance of someone else recognising you for me to make any such commitment.'

Reluctantly, Anne nodded. He had just voiced her worst fear, but at the same time had planted the seed of an idea. If Tom kept her secret for now, she could arrange to be out in the field when the crew actually arrived. She would have kept her part of the bargain, justifying Sam's faith in her. Once Tom Callander had his precious locations, there was no need for her to be involved further.

'Then we're agreed,' she said. 'I help you find your locations and you keep my secret.'

'Until my crew arrives,' he cautioned, regarding her with frank suspicion. Did he guess what was in her mind now? If they never found suitable locations, the film crew might never arrive at all.

'You wouldn't be scheming, would you?' he asked.

Anne was aware of a warm flush settling over her cheeks, but ducked her head before he saw it. 'Of course not. I told you I'll do my job, and I will.'

She didn't add that she would do it so well that he would never even contemplate bringing expensive equipment into the places she planned to show him. He wanted the real outback. Very well, he would have it—if it killed him.

CHAPTER THREE

SHE was up to something—Tom knew it. The sixth sense which had made him uncannily successful in countless business deals was operating on maximum now. Every instinct told him to beware of Deanne Flame, or Anne Fleming, or whatever she currently called herself.

At the same time, his mind was filled with a vision of a petite, chestnut-haired creature with hazel eyes that reflected the glow of the outback at sunset. Could she possibly be the same woman who had sailed past him on the set all those years ago, in a black dress as skimpy as decency allowed, her face overlaid with so much make-up that her youthful glow was almost, but not quite, extinguished?

Tom made himself remember that day. It was the first time Joanna's daughter had been on the set when he was around, and the sight of her had made him feel as if he'd been king-hit. Seeing her lithe body, barely decent in the skimpy black dress, had sent his hormones raging. Yet there was more to it than mere chemistry. When he looked more closely, he felt sure there was a vulnerable teenager under the sophisticated trappings. Then they were introduced, and her haughty manner had swept away any such delusions. She was a clone of her mother, heaven help her. Right down to the callous disregard for anyone but herself, as his father's death had proved.

When had she turned into a hard-working geologist, buried in the middle of nowhere? Why was she here? Women like Joanna and her daughter never did anything unless there was a pay-off in it. Was Anne hoping to marry a rich grazier, or the owner of a goldmine? A jolt passed through Tom at the idea and he cursed under his breath. There he went again, reacting at the thought of her with another man when it was none of his business.

He raked stiff fingers through his hair. It was time he remembered who she was and why she was off-limits to him. Between them, she and her mother had killed his father—or at least their actions had caused Howard Callander's death. And Anne had admitted to him that she had not the slightest regret. Well, she would have more than a few before he was finished with her. She owed him, and today he intended to start collecting.

His features were grim as he finished packing. Dawn hadn't yet lightened the sky, but he had arranged to get an early start to beat the midday heat. The Deanne of old would never have been ready for such an early start. Tom's mouth twisted into an ironic smile as he wondered if he would have to haul her out of bed. Now *that* might prove interesting.

Normally the thought of trekking into the bush for a couple of days would have filled Anne with excitement. Even after five years, the thrill of exploring new places was still strong. But this trip filled her with dread. Tom Callander's dislike was too obvious, and she had a feeling it wasn't only due to their ill-fated first meeting. But what else could there be?

Without conscious thought, she had tied her hair back and dressed plainly in jeans and a shirt. She didn't want him thinking of her as anything other than a guide while they were away. Not that she had any cause to worry, she told herself with a rueful glance in the mirror.

She knew the sort of woman that attracted men like Tom. Hadn't she attended enough studio parties in her teens to know that a youthful glow and a sheen of sunscreen weren't enough? Which was just as well, since the point of this expedition was to end his stay here as quickly as possible.

The first morning rays of the sun were staining the sky with coral when she heard him drive up. They had agreed to travel in a company-supplied four-wheel-drive vehicle that waited outside her quarters.

She had personally checked it over, and the field gear included every item they could possibly need, from puncture and tyre repair kits to spare hoses, fuses, bulbs, fan-belt, radiator, brake and clutch fluids, as well as tow-ropes, axe, spade and jumper leads. Miscellaneous items included emergency rations, plastic bags, bucket and tape to cope with any contingency.

The vehicle itself was equipped with a water tank, extra fuel tank and battery, bull bar and radio on which she could call the flying doctor or Australia-wide via satellite. A small portable refrigerator completed the inventory.

Tom looked surprised when she opened the door before he could knock. 'Good, you're already up,' he said shortly.

'Didn't you think I would be?'

His look told her what he thought, and she cringed inwardly. Even now, he still thought of her as a clone of her mother. Joanna had never seen the sun come up in her life, unless it was because she hadn't been to bed the night before.

He accepted the ziped holdall which held her personal needs, and tossed it into the back with the rest of the equipment. He had already added his own case to the pile, she noticed. Then he looked around. 'Is this all you're taking?' he asked.

Provoked in spite of herself, Anne said with heavy sarcasm, 'Oh, gee, I forgot my day-and-night make-up kit and my ten pairs of false eyelashes!'

A muscle worked in his jaw, but he contained himself with an obvious effort. 'Very amusing. If you've finished with the one-liners, we can get started.'

But instead of climbing into the passenger door he held open for her, she slammed it shut, narrowly missing his fingers. 'We aren't going anywhere until we get a couple of things straight,' she told him.

He leaned against the vehicle and regarded her with wry amusement. 'Indeed? What might they be?'

'You seem to think that Anne Fleming is some kind of role I'm playing and if you dig deeply enough you'll come to the real me, which, for some reason, you dislike intensely. Although what I've done to you, I don't know.'

She tailed off as a curious glint came into his eyes, like the light of battle. His long fingers flexed as if he would like nothing better than to feel them around her neck. She shuddered involuntarily, but all he said was, 'Go ahead, I'm listening.'

The sight of him so obviously furious with her had siphoned off some of her own anger. Was she crazy, going bush with a man who plainly hated her? It couldn't be because of her behaviour on a movie set years ago, so what was the reason? 'I—I just want you to treat me the way you'd treat any other woman you have to work with,' she stammered.

'No problem.' He took a step forward and wrapped her in an inescapable embrace, his hands warm on her back as he crushed her against him.

With no time to prepare, she was swept along on a tidal wave of erotic sensations more powerful than anything she'd ever experienced. Hot breath invaded her mouth as he forced her lips apart and plundered her mouth with a skill that left her clinging weakly to him.

Summoning her strength, she pushed him away. 'I hate you,' she snapped through gritted teeth.

The derision in his expression made her want to scratch his eyes out. 'You ask me to treat you like any other woman, then object when I do. Which is it to be?' he asked with feigned innocence.

'You knew perfectly well what I meant. You had no right to do that,' she seethed. 'It seems that the casting couch is alive and well in your world.'

'It's your world too, no matter how you try to dodge the issue,' he reminded her. 'But rest assured I have no need of such devices to keep myself in female companionship, so your honour is safe on this journey. But I'd word your challenges more precisely in future.'

Before she could word a scathing reply, he climbed into the driver's side of the car and started the motor. She was left with no choice but to get in, keeping as much distance between them as she possibly could.

He was hateful beyond belief, thinking he could behave with her as he did with other women. She wasn't part of his world, no matter how he tried to drag her back into it. Her mother would say she was making a mountain out of a molehill, and possibly she was, but she couldn't dismiss his kiss as lightly as he seemed able to do.

She sneaked a sidelong glance at him. He seemed to have forgotten her already and was giving his whole attention to the driving. Covertly, Anne studied him. His hands rested lightly on the steering-wheel as if controlling the powerful vehicle by will-power alone. His lips were pursed in a soundless whistle as if he was responding to a tune running through his head. The kiss might never have happened, as far as he was concerned.

For her, the memory was too vivid for comfort, although she tried to match his indifference outwardly. But her mouth felt sensitised, as if the contact had bruised her lips. Her body still held the imprint of his, and a shudder ran through her. Anyone would think she had enjoyed the kiss, when it had been an insult from beginning to end.

She was giving the whole thing too much importance, she told herself. She had thrown down a gauntlet, but she would know better next time. It

would be a long time before she gave Tom
Callander an excuse to kiss her again. Nor would
she give him the satisfaction of seeing how strongly
it preyed on her mind. If he could be indifferent,
so could she. It was the only way to prove to
him...to herself...that his kiss hadn't mattered
one bit.

'What would you like to see first? What part of
the goldfields?' she asked as he shot her a speculative look.

'I thought we agreed to work our way up through
Broad Arrow and Menzies, then to Kookynie and
Leonora, then proceed on foot.'

She cursed herself for forgetting that they had
mapped out a route only a couple of days before.
What was happening to her? She was usually so
organised and efficient.

She made an effort to concentrate as they drove
out of town along the tree-lined streets of
Kalgoorlie, which slumbered in the early morning.

She had read somewhere that the city had more
species of trees than anywhere else in Western
Australia, planted to provide shade and control dust
storms, so she occupied herself by identifying as
many species as she could. But after acacias, salmon
gums and gimlet gums, she gave up. Her mind
wasn't on the surroundings. It was on the man
sitting beside her. For some reason he drew her attention as a magnet draws metal filings. If only
there was some way she could get out of this trip,
but she could see none.

Their first stop, Broad Arrow, had once been a
thriving community of over two thousand people,
but it now boasted a population of only twenty.

Tom pulled up outside the one remaining hotel and reached for his still camera.

'I remember seeing this place in *The Nickel Queen*,' he told Anne.

She remembered the film, the first feature film ever made in the state. 'The stone railway station was still standing then,' she added. 'Do you know how Broad Arrow came by its name?'

'Something to do with a prospector leaving a trail of arrows on the ground for his mates to follow, wasn't it?'

She nodded. 'When the town was gazetted, they tried to rename it Kurawah, but it never caught on.'

'The original is much more picturesque.' He aimed his camera at the remaining buildings and snapped several pictures in quick succession. The long, low hotel with its sheltering veranda looked like a relic of a bygone age, as in fact it was.

The rich red soil seemed painted in ochre, too brilliant in colour to be real. Anne had passed this way many times before and normally enjoyed it. But this time it was an effort to stand by patiently while Tom snapped several more pictures. At this rate, they'd be out here forever.

When they were under way again, headed for the town of Menzies, she turned to Tom. 'You're pretty handy with a still camera,' she remarked.

He glanced sideways at her before returning his attention to the road. 'I was taking pictures before I could write,' he explained.

Anne braced herself as they jolted over an uneven patch. 'I take it that's a figure of speech?'

His sober gaze returned to her. 'No, it's the truth. As a child, I was dyslexic, but nobody woke up to the fact in the beginning and the problem hadn't had as much publicity as it has since then. My teachers thought I was stupid and, quite frankly, I believed them.'

It was hard to accept that someone as self-assured as Tom Callander could ever have believed such a thing. 'So what happened?' she asked.

'I was given a cheap camera for my birthday and started winning photographic competitions with my still pictures. This convinced me that there was nothing wrong with my brain, it was my reading that was faulty. I decided I wasn't stupid, and then was lucky enough to meet a teacher who understood my problem and how to handle it. I never looked back.'

'I can see why you've never lost your enthusiasm for still photography,' Anne remarked.

He swerved to avoid a pothole in the road, then went on. 'I still prefer it to film, even though I make movies for a living. Film-making is a team effort, whereas photography is an art form, and it can be pursued alone.'

Her surprised look flew to him. 'You prefer being alone?'

'Sometimes. Composing a picture is like painting one. You need solitude to determine the essence of your subject before you can capture it for posterity.'

He fell silent, and she wondered if he had said more than he meant to. She had a feeling that his childhood handicap wasn't something he talked about very readily, and she felt unwillingly flattered that he had confided in her. She almost wished he hadn't. It made him seem much more human than she wanted him to be.

He decided to stop for a break in Menzies, once a sizeable town with a population of over five thousand people. Now there were less than a hundred, and old mine excavations were scattered around the landscape like trenches from a long-ago battlefield.

At the sight of the town's imposing brick town hall, Tom's eyes gleamed. 'I must get a shot of that,' he decided.

He was behaving as if they were ordinary sight-seers, Anne realised with a surge of resentment. Had he forgotten that she wasn't here by choice? 'It must be one of the most photographed buildings in the goldfields,' she reminded him acidly.

'Not with you in front of it.' Ignoring her objections, he steered her to the arched entrance of the red-brick building with its lofty tower. 'Now look up at the clock.'

In spite of her irritation, she was forced to smile, earning a frown from him. 'Now what's so funny?' he demanded.

It was a pleasure to know something he didn't. 'There is no clock,' she explained. 'The ship bringing it out from England sank and the clock was lost. It was never replaced.'

Instead of being annoyed, he looked upwards and gave a rueful grin when he saw that she was right. His smile made something twist inside her in reluctant response, but she fought it down. He had made her come on this trip. The last thing she wanted was to start softening towards him, a prospect which filled her with dismay.

The click of a shutter drew her attention. 'Got it. That wistful, bitter-sweet expression is just right

for this place. A haunted look for a haunted past.'
His eyes narrowed. 'But I have a hunch you weren't
thinking of the past, were you?'

Admitting that it was Tom himself who had provoked her haunted expression would be foolhardy
in the extreme. A man like him wouldn't hesitate
to use whatever power he perceived he possessed.
'My wistful look was for the coffee I was promised
when we got here,' said Anne with deliberate
flippancy.

His eyes became shuttered and he holstered his
camera. 'Very well, coffee it is, then. Where's the
best place to find it?'

She was withdrawn and quiet during their coffee
break. If Tom noticed he made no comment,
spreading maps and guide books out on the table
to study. 'I'd like to spend a few hours around
Niagara and Kookynie,' he said after a long in-
spection of the maps. 'Kookynie looks like a ready-
made film set.'

'The road's pretty rough, and there's nothing
much left of the township,' she warned him.

He gave her a heavy-lidded look. 'Not afraid of
a few ghosts, are you, Anne?'

If she was, they were the ghosts of her own past,
but she didn't say so. Already it looked as if her
plan to scare him off filming in the area by taking
him to the most rugged spots was falling apart. He
seemed to revel in the rough conditions, as if he
enjoyed testing himself against the elements. He
played to win, she recalled. But where there were
winners, there were usually losers, she acknowledged to herself. Would she be among them this
time?

'No, I'm not afraid of ghosts,' she answered belatedly. 'If I was, I wouldn't be doing this kind of work.'

Tom cupped his hands around his coffee-cup and regarded her through the tendrils of steam spiralling off it. 'Do you come out here alone very often?' he asked.

'Most of the time. It doesn't bother me, provided I'm well prepared. And I always tell someone where I'm going and when I should be back.'

He looked out of the café window at the endless expanse of open scrubland that encroached on the town boundaries. 'Have you ever got lost?'

She looked down at the table. 'I'm blessed with a good sense of direction and I take care to note landmarks such as unusual vegetation, track branches, windmills, dams, that kind of thing. And I carry a compass.'

He took a sip of coffee. 'It's a long way from the film world, isn't it?'

Her finger traced the Paisley design of the vinyl tablecloth. 'I thought so, but evidently it isn't far enough,' she said drily.

Anger darkened his eyes to teal. 'Still as big a snob as your mother, aren't you? Is it me personally or any film producer who rates that look of disgust that comes over your face whenever the industry is mentioned?'

Tears shimmered dangerously close to the surface. 'You made it personal by forcing me to come with you. I like my life the way it was—is—away from the limelight. Is it too much to ask, simply to be left alone?'

She jumped to her feet, rattling the cups and sending coffee sloshing across the table. Tom moved aside to avoid it, then had to stop and pay their bill. By the time he was able to follow her outside, she was resting in the shade of the vehicle, her outburst firmly under control again.

He opened the car doors to let the heat escape, then paused beside her. 'Running away from something doesn't usually solve it,' he told her.

She met his searching gaze defiantly. 'Who says I'm running away from anything?'

'You're obviously hiding out here.' He gestured at the arid expanse around them, dotted with disused mines. 'There can't be much to offer a woman like you out here.'

Anne vaulted into the high passenger-seat of the car, having given up the tussle to drive several stops ago. 'Which just goes to show how little you know me!' she retorted.

'Oh, but I will,' he said softly. 'By the time this trip is over, we should know one another very well indeed.'

Her nervous look flickered to his face, but the hooded eyes revealed nothing. 'What do you mean?' she queried.

This time he did look at her, but his blue gaze was as fathomless as the ocean depths. 'Alone in the wilderness with no one else to talk to, we're bound to get to know each other better, wouldn't you say? I'm interested in you, Anne. What brought you here, why you stay. It's quite important to me.'

'I can't imagine why it should be.'

He slammed his door shut, gesturing for her to do the same before gunning the powerful motor. 'Can't you, Anne? I'm sure you could if you tried.'

'Well, I can't,' she snapped back, tired of his crazy guessing game. If there was something she was supposed to know, why didn't he come right out and ask her instead of teasing her with hints?

As he drove out of Menzies on to the north road towards the Kookynie turn-off, she racked her brains, but could think of no connection between them which would account for his strange attitude.

His father, the well-known producer Howard Callander, had produced several of her mother's films. It was even reputed that they had had an affair some years after Anne's father died. Somehow, Anne doubted it, because her mother had the annoying habit of confiding in her daughter, sometimes telling her more than was good for her young ears. By her early teens Anne had heard most of the details of her mother's love life, even though she tried to discourage the confidences. And even if Joanna had somehow broken Howard Callander's heart—which was not impossible, knowing Joanna—Anne was hardly to blame.

She gave a restless sigh. She could agonise all day and still not come up with an explanation, and Tom was unlikely to enlighten her until he was good and ready.

The car gave a jolt and slithered sideways as they turned off the main road on to the rocky side road which led to Niagara Dam and the township of Kookynie.

Tom wrestled with the wheel. When they were under control again, he asked, 'Mind if we stop for a look at Niagara?'

Anne gave a careless shrug. 'You're the boss, at least of what we see and do out here.'

His eyebrow arched into a speculative line. 'Remember that when we come to a disagreement, won't you?'

He wouldn't let her forget it, she was sure. In any contest of wills, she had no doubt who would win. But he wouldn't find the contest entirely one-sided—she would see to it.

In this rebellious frame of mind, she offered to wait in the vehicle while he took some photographs of the country around Niagara Dam.

She was startled when he wrenched open the passenger door and lifted her lightly down from her seat. 'Sorry, sweetheart—I'm going to need you this time.'

'For what?'

'A stand-in, to give the pictures some scale and perspective. Everything's so darned big out here that it'll be difficult to convey an idea of its size when I get the pictures home.'

The thought of being in front of his camera sent a combination of fear and excitement flooding through her. She hadn't minded posing for the earlier picture, which was no more than a tourist snapshot. This was somehow different. The fear she understood; she had promised herself never to be beguiled into posing for a camera again. But the excitement could only be because Tom was the person asking. 'No, I'm sorry, it isn't part of our deal,' she said firmly, although her voice shook with emotion.

Tom gave an impatient sigh. 'I'm not asking you to take your clothes off, for pity's sake. All you have to do is stand in front of the scenery like a store dummy. Is that asking too much?'

'N-no, I suppose not.'

'Then for crying out loud, get on with it!'

The rocky red sides of the dam were strangely eroded with many shallow caves and deep pools of shade. The effect was strange and eerie. It was easy to imagine it when the dam was being built with the help of hundreds of camels bearing huge loads of concrete for the dam wall.

The falls themselves were tame compared with their American namesake, but substantial by gold-fields standards. The sound of tumbling water reached Anne as she posed in front of a shallow cave while Tom fiddled with the settings on his camera.

'Relax—you're supposed to be a young woman in love,' he told her.

'I thought I was supposed to be a store dummy.'

He ignored the taunt. 'The woman in this scene is madly in love and on the verge of marrying her young man, when they get caught up in the affairs of a local Aboriginal tribesman,' he explained. 'This is their secret trysting place.'

As he outlined the scene he had in mind, Anne began to envisage it, almost against her will. The eerie splendour of the place, the birdlife and the cascading water created a romantic atmosphere. It was easy to imagine young lovers adopting it as their own.

She was so lost in the image that she was surprised when Tom murmured into her ear, 'You can relax now, sweetheart.'

She looked up at him in dazed surprise. 'Did you get everything you wanted?' she asked.

His eyes softened and his mouth hovered tantalisingly close. 'No one gets everything they want, but I got more than I expected this time.'

She felt herself sliding under the cool waters of the dam, clasping him against her as they swirled down and down, his fevered body pressing against her while his seeking mouth claimed hers in a kiss that went on and on until they reached the shadowy depths.

With a startled cry, she ducked under his arm and moved away, her face hot as she realised what she was doing. The picture of them swimming together in the dam had been entirely in her mind. Tom hadn't even touched her except in her own traitorous thoughts. What was she doing, harbouring such fantasies?

'What is it, Anne? Is it the heat?'

She pressed her palms to her fiery cheeks. 'No, it isn't really hot for out here. I didn't like posing for you.'

'It looked as if you liked it a great deal,' he countered, his tone frosty. 'Did I awaken old memories? Are you afraid you'll come to your senses and realise what you gave up to come here?'

'I gave up nothing of value,' she snapped. 'The truth is, posing for you reminded me of what it's like to be a commodity, a piece of fodder for a camera. I'm glad I'm not part of it any more.'

Thunderclouds gathered in his eyes and, too late, she realised what a challenge her words represented. For a moment she had forgotten that film was his life. 'I'm sorry, I spoke out of turn,' she said, clasping her hands together.

'We may as well know where we stand with each other,' he said with icy dispassion. 'As it happens, I don't believe a word of it. I know what I saw through that viewfinder, and it wasn't a woman who hates the camera. For those few minutes you *were* Katie Dooley, and you can't deny it.'

Anne stared at him, stunned. It was true. While she posed beside the dam, she had seen herself as the girl in the film, waiting for her lover. But it was no more than the mood of the moment, a combination of the exotic scenery and—yes, she had to admit it—Tom's presence. It didn't mean she wanted any part of the film he was making.

'You're wrong,' she said with harsh finality. 'As an actress, I'm a first-rate geologist, and the sooner you accept it, the better.'

A frown of disagreement settled over his even features. 'You may accept it, for some reason, but I don't. You may think you're some kind of career nun with the outback as your convent, but it doesn't change who you really are.'

It was an act of despair, fuelled by rage at his persistence and the awful fear that he might be right. Before she knew what she was doing, she launched herself at him and beat at his broad chest with doubled fists. 'I hate you, do you hear? I hate you!' she railed at him.

Tom caught her fists and pulled her arms down, pinning them behind her back with one hand. As she looked up at him in helpless fury, the tears dried on her face. He gave a throaty laugh, and satisfaction gleamed in his eyes. 'At last,' he said softly. 'Now we're getting somewhere.'

CHAPTER FOUR

WITH her hands pinned behind her, Anne could only wait, trembling, in Tom's grasp, wondering what he meant when he said they were 'getting somewhere'.

But abruptly his hold slackened and he turned his back, striding to the lake's edge before he stopped and stared out at the glass-smooth water.

Should she follow him and apologise for her outburst? It was appalling behaviour from someone who prided herself on her cool, scientific demeanour. No man had driven her to attack him physically before, and she wasn't sure what had impelled her this time.

His insistence that she belonged in the film world was infuriating, but surely not enough to justify her behaviour? What was it about Tom Callander that undermined every one of her defences?

After a few minutes he came back, his face set and impassive. 'Ready to proceed?' he asked.

She took a deep breath. 'First, I want to apologise. I don't know what came over me just now.'

His blue eyes changed to cool grey. 'I've dealt with worse displays of temperament before,' he assured her.

She chewed her lower lip unhappily. 'But not from me. A geologist is supposed to be scientific and detached, not ... the way I acted.'

The grey-blue gaze lightened a fraction. 'Even a geologist is allowed to be human once in a while. Would I sound like a bad script if I said you looked beautiful when you were angry?'

'Pretty bad,' she agreed, but a flush crept up her skin at the compliment. During her outburst her hair had sprung loose from its clip and she gathered it back into place, trying to quieten the butterflies fluttering inside her. His words were empty, meaningless, typical of the film world where strangers called each other 'darling' or 'sweetheart' and it meant nothing.

She tensed as he reached out and tucked a strand of hair back behind her ear. His hand brushed her cheek, then dropped to his side. A weight settled on her chest suddenly, and it was an effort to summon her voice. 'Shouldn't we get going?' she asked.

The curious look she had intercepted when he touched her vanished as quickly as it appeared. 'You're right. We have a lot of ground to cover before nightfall.'

Nightfall. They would spend it somewhere out in the bush together. Just the two of them. It hadn't concerned her when they planned the expedition. Now the outback didn't seem big enough to contain the two of them, alone.

Tom opened the map and spread it across the bonnet of the four-wheel-drive. 'We can stop for lunch at Niagara township,' he said, stabbing the map with a forefinger.

The change of subject made nervous laughter bubble up inside her, and he shot her a questioning look. 'Did I say something amusing?'

'We could have had lunch in Niagara in 1900.' She shaded her eyes and pointed to a ruined mud-brick chimney visible from where they stood. 'That's all that remains of the township. It only ever had two main streets, and where they intersected a hotel stood on each corner.'

'I see.' With a self-deprecating smile, he returned to the map. 'Before I make any more plans, is there anything left of Kookynie?'

Anne nodded. 'The Grand Hotel is still standing. It's a striking place, built around the turn of the century.'

She felt no obligation to add that she loved the old hotel, or that on the way they would pass some wonderful rock formations which would appeal to his photographer's eye. Let him find them for himself, or miss out.

Trust him to spot them unerringly. Was there no way she could thwart his plans? He seemed to be one step ahead of her no matter what she did. In frustrated silence, she followed as he photographed the rich red earth scattered with old mine workings and low scrub. When he had enough pictures, he led her up a steep climb to the top of a breakaway which afforded a good view of the arid plains.

He reached for her hand to help her up the last few yards. His grip was firm and his fingers curled comfortably around hers. Was it her imagination, or did his hand linger in hers for a fraction longer than was necessary? Definitely her imagination, she decided, tugging free with such force that she almost slid back down the breakaway.

'Thank goodness you have quick reflexes,' she said as he grabbed her just in time.

His gaze was thoughtful, the blue eyes grey again as he steadied her. 'Easy, honey. No view's worth a broken leg.'

There it was again, another empty endearment sliding from those generous lips. If she wasn't careful, she would start thinking he meant them. She turned towards the view. 'As you can see, I didn't mislead you,' she said.

'Not about this.' Tom busied himself capturing the scene on film. This time he didn't ask her to pose for him, and she didn't know whether to be glad or sorry.

They stopped for lunch at the Grand Hotel in Kookynie, once a thriving mining town. Now, like so many other centres in the goldfields, it subsisted with a handful of people, although petrol was available and a caravan parking facility was doing good business.

Tom became engrossed in conversation with one of the local prospectors, while Anne was content to sip her cold shandy in silence.

Try as she might to think of other things, her thoughts kept drifting to Tom. Propped against the bar with his bush hat pushed far back on his head, he looked utterly at home in the country pub. He looked unnervingly masculine, from the tips of his dust-streaked boots to the metallic sheen of his hair.

At this moment he looked more like the boss of a prosperous sheep station than the owner of the film studio. Anne's heart thudded in her chest. If only he *was* a farmer, there would be no reason to keep a rein on her emotions which kept threatening to spin out of control.

But he wasn't a farmer, and she would do well to keep it in mind. In his business, fact and fantasy were intertwined. Endearments were cheap and sex was a means to an end.

She remembered attending a wrap party at the end of one of her mother's films and seeing one of the lead actors on the arm of a teenage starlet. 'But he's married,' she told her mother in disgust.

'His motto is "why settle for one apple when you can have the whole tree?"' her mother had explained somewhat apologetically. Anne knew she could never feel the way they did about love. Like her father, she dreamed of a love 'till death us do part'.

Vincent Fleming had loved her mother passionately. If he had lived, Anne was sure her mother would have been different. Certainly Vincent would have fought tooth and nail to preserve the relationship he believed in.

More than anything, Anne wanted to be like him. Given her upbringing, it was inevitable that someone like Tom Callander should attract her. But she would be a fool to give in to it.

Tom slid into the seat opposite her and dropped a notebook on to the table. 'You look positively grim. Was I neglecting you?'

'Of course not. This is a business trip and——'

'And you won't let me forget it for a minute,' he said heavily. 'As it happens, I got some wonderful background for the film. The old prospector tells me his grandfather was working at Cue the day the first train came in.' He consulted his notes. 'He described the excitement as if he'd been there himself—bands playing, flags waving, then the train arriving with its VIP passengers. Riding up front was Herbert Hoover, waving the American flag.'

'Shades of things to come,' murmured Anne. Almost against her will, she found herself sharing his vision. 'Are you going to use it in your film?'

He nodded, his eyes glittering with enthusiasm which turned them from ice-blue to the sheen of a summer sea with the sun glistening on the waves. 'Apparently Hoover used to visit the Gentlemen's Club in Cue.'

'I've read about it. Later it became a laundry. These days it's merely a picturesque ruin.'

He leaned forward, pushing the notes aside to grasp her hands. 'But we could recreate it just as it used to be.'

Clasped in his firm grip, it was difficult to remember that his passion was reserved for his subject. It had nothing to do with a wish to touch her. Still, she let out a taut breath when he realised what he was doing and released her. 'Now you understand why I came out to soak it all up for myself. You can't do this kind of research in books.'

This time she had no difficulty in agreeing with him. 'My job is the same. I can spend hours in the office trying to establish the prospects for a mine, the type of rocks and structures which could be present, resolving the mine's current standing with the Department of Mines and so on. But I don't really know what's out there until I make a field visit and locate the actual ore-bodies.'

It was the most she'd told him about her work so far, and he gave a low whistle. 'You're a remarkable woman, Anne Fleming.'

'Because I don't mind getting my hands dirty? Or because I have a brain and like to use it?' She was willing to bet that none of the starlets of his acquaintance could boast much of either.

'Because you have a passion,' he said unexpectedly. 'You do what you love, and you love what you do.'

'Is it so unusual?'

'It is in my line of work, where money is usually the overriding factor.'

'Yet *you* love what you do.' His enthusiasm when he talked about his work was transparent.

He took a swallow of cold beer and reached for his hat. 'There are exceptions to every rule, sweetheart. Come on, it's time we got under way again. I want to see Leonora while the light's still good.'

Once they were back on the main road, the town of Leonora was only an hour's drive away. It was mid-afternoon when they reached it and Tom was unsheathing his camera almost before they had stopped rolling.

'It's a pity we weren't here before noon,' Anne told him. The old-style covered walkway along the west side of the main street was in the best light then.

Tom wasn't fazed and shot a whole reel of film around the town, commenting on novel items like an old hotel sign which offered meals and beds for two shillings and sixpence. 'When you consider that's about twenty-five of our cents, it's not a bad deal,' he commented.

Together they made the half-hour climb up the rocky peak which overlooked the town and distant bushland. At sunset they could have photographed the unique 'galloping shadow' which overtook the landscape faster than walking pace.

'I'd need a movie camera to do it justice,' Tom said when Anne mentioned it. 'But I might use it in the actual film.'

He was more interested in visiting the nearby town of Gwalia, headquarters of the famous Sons of Gwalia Mine which Herbert Hoover had managed at the turn of the century.

Most of the houses were made of corrugated iron, rubble and junk. Tom's camera clicked incessantly as he captured it all for later assessment. He was enthralled by the old wood-hauling locomotives and wagons, wondering aloud if they could be used as props.

'This is a veritable goldmine!' he enthused, then wondered why Anne burst out laughing. 'Oh, yes, I see.'

Catching her hand, he hurried her to the historical gallery located in the original 1898 mine office, and an hour flew by as they pored over the collection of artefacts, mining gear and samples of gold on display. If the gallery hadn't closed at four, Anne was sure he would have spent another hour among the displays.

Trying not to be affected by his enthusiasm, she made herself remember that by giving him what he wanted she was sealing her own fate.

The more she showed him, the keener he became to bring his film crew to the area. If she was to convince him that filming in the goldfields was impracticable, she needed to act quickly.

'We should start choosing a campsite soon,' she advised. 'Some of the country around here's pretty rugged. It's better to make camp before sunset.'

'I'm in your hands,' he told her with a lop-sided smile that made her wish there was some other way to achieve her aim. His nearness played havoc with her emotions. Heaven knew how she would cope alone with him in the bush.

She would cope because she had to, she told herself decisively. As long as Tom was around, her whole lifestyle was in jeopardy—and not just her lifestyle, she admitted reluctantly to herself. He was dangerously attractive. What would happen if she lost her head over a man like him she knew only too well.

It would be wonderful for a while. She had no doubt that he could be an expert and sensitive lover. If the rumours about him were true, he was a regular Don Juan. He was also successful and assured, no doubt willing to lay every luxury at her feet. She had seen it happen around her too many times, to her mother and to other actresses.

The crunch would come when he tired of her, or someone younger and prettier threw herself at his feet. Then she would become an apple in a tree of them, to be sampled and discarded in favour of the next juicy offering.

'No way!'

She was unaware of having voiced the denial until Tom said, 'I beg your pardon?'

Flustered, she felt her face grow hot. 'Sorry, I was thinking aloud.'

'I'd better not ask what prompted such an aggressive refusal,' he said with a wry grin as he led the way back to the car.

The Leonora to Wiluna road was actually a rough bush track which became virtually impassable after rain. As Tom drove, Anne agonised over her next step. She could direct him to the left, to the Terraces, which was rugged but accessible country. Or they could turn right, through a series of gates and fences, to an area of mountainous wash-outs, deep sand and tyre-slashing tree roots. It seemed underhanded, but what choice did she have?

'Let's take that track,' she said, gesturing to a barely discernible pair of tyre marks leading into the bush to their right.

Tom frowned. 'I thought the Terraces were off to the left.'

'You'll have a better view of them this way, although not until morning. But there are some interesting old workings out this way.'

He shrugged and spun the wheel. 'As I said, I'm in your hands.'

Several grinding miles later Anne wondered what she'd got them into. Several times her head careered off the roof of the cabin as they hit a particularly sump-grinding series of tree roots. Although Tom drove with a skill that surprised her, considering he was new to these conditions, there were so many obstacles that it was impossible to avoid them all.

After she had opened and closed yet another stock gate to allow him to drive through, she climbed wearily back on board. 'I think we should stop for the night,' she told him.

'I was wondering when you'd give in,' he said grimly.

Her startled gaze flew to his face, which looked piratical in the late afternoon shadows. 'What do you mean?' she queried.

'I think you knew exactly what you were doing when you directed me down this road—if you can call it a road. What I want to know is why.'

'I told you. The scenery's interesting and——'

'And all we've seen so far are gates, fences and windmills, so don't give me that bull about the scenery.'

He slammed on the brakes and the car jolted to a halt, throwing her against his side. She was instantly aware of the hardness of his body and the masculine scent of him, tinged with the faint reminder of his after-shave lotion.

Despite everything standing between them, she felt an almost overwhelming temptation to rest against him and feel his arms around her. What was happening to her? She had never felt so confused by her feelings before.

Alarmed at her uninhibited reaction, she pulled away, grabbing the door-handle to lever herself upright. 'You make it sound as if I have an ulterior motive for choosing this route,' she said, trying to sound wounded at the very suggestion.

His laughter was a low growl that lacked any hint of amusement. 'Oh, you do, lady, you do. Maybe it's your way of paying me back for being who I am.'

At least he didn't suspect the real reason, she thought. 'You can hardly blame me for doing my

job too well,' she said, sounding convincingly
offended.

'True enough. But if I find this is part of some
scheme of yours, by thunder, I'll make you regret
it.'

Taking refuge in humour, Anne managed a smile.
'Are you threatening a poor helpless female, Mr
Callander?'

His lazy look encompassed the fullness of her
breasts, which were emphasised by the seatbelt
slashing across them. 'Female you certainly are. But
poor and helpless, I doubt it. No one who survives
alone in these conditions can be called helpless.'

Yet she had never felt more helpless and vulnerable than she did at this moment, cocooned in
the small cabin with a man whose very existence
set her senses on fire.

What a fool she was, bringing them to such a
lonely spot and thinking she could control the situation. She could barely control the hammering of
her heart against her ribs. It was a wonder Tom
couldn't hear it.

He gave a long-suffering sigh and forced open
his door, putting his weight against it to counter
the angle at which they were parked. 'Now we're
here, we may as well take a look around.'

She joined him outside, and her heart sank as
she saw how rugged the surroundings were. It was
the sort of country which should properly be explored by foot. They would be lucky to be able to
drive out again in one piece.

But that worry could be postponed until
morning. Of more pressing concern was where they
should camp. There was no reliable water for miles,

so it was just as well that they had ample supplies on board. 'It's quite pretty in a wild sort of way,' she said over-brightly, to compensate for her own growing apprehension.

'If we ever make it out of here to talk about it,' he said, echoing her fears.

'You wanted authentic locations for your film.'

He gave her a look of studied disbelief. 'You call this authentic? How could a place like this even have a history, when human beings can't get to it?'

She sobered. 'You'd be surprised at some of the places the old goldminers managed to get to, and they didn't have four-wheel-drive vehicles. They came on foot, pushing barrows or rolling barrels filled with their worldly goods, but they got here.'

Tom thrust a hand through his hair, which glinted like old gold in the afternoon light. The dark highlights at his temples stood out like lightning flashes. 'So there really are the remains of old workings out here?'

'Very likely.' It was a safe assumption. Most of this country had been scoured for gold at some time during the last century.

'Very likely,' he repeated with heavy sarcasm. 'In other words, you don't know. Why *did* you bring me on this wild-goose chase, Anne?'

'I told you, it isn't a wild-goose chase, it's——'

Suspicion clouded his gaze as he interrupted her. 'It may not be a wild-goose chase to you—I'm sure you know exactly what we're doing. But I warn you, you won't get away with whatever it is. Ask any of my associates and they'll tell you I can be hellishly hard to get along with when I'm crossed.'

Anne didn't need to ask anyone to know he was telling the truth, and she shivered as she imagined what he would do if he found out what she was really up to.

Somehow she had to convince him that her motives were above board, even while she dissuaded him from bringing a film crew to the area. Suddenly she was glad that the night stood between her and facing the issue next day.

Setting up camp kept them too busy for further speculation about her motives. The four-wheel-drive was fitted with a car-top tent which stowed into a roof rack during travel, then unfolded into a substantial lean-to arrangement.

Sleeping quarters on top of the car were accessible by ladder, with a large living area down below. Although the goldfields were too dry for mosquitoes, the windows were screened against insects, and there was a fluorescent light.

'All the comforts of home,' Tom said, unrolling his sleeping-bag on top of a camp stretcher. He had insisted that Anne take the more comfortable car-top bed, although she had tried to argue that he was the client and she the employee. He didn't seem to welcome the reminder.

'Look at it this way: your honour will be safer up there. You can pull the ladder up if you want to.'

'I hadn't given it a thought,' she denied, although the thought of spending the night with him in such confined quarters *had* occupied her mind.

Where was her professionalism? Travelling with other male geologists was commonplace and shouldn't have such an effect on her. Was it because she couldn't retreat into shop talk with Tom? He already knew more about her past than any of her associates, and the awareness left her feeling strangely vulnerable.

'There's still time to look around before dark,' Tom announced once their camp was set up.

'I don't know. This is wild country. All the bush looks the same after a while.'

'Are you scared I'll get lost—or scared that I won't?' he asked shrewdly.

She managed a careless shrug. 'It hardly matters to me, either way.'

'In that case, let's go.'

She was supposed to be the guide, but Tom frequently strode ahead of her, forcing her to trot to keep up.

Far from being deterred by the rugged country, he seemed enthralled by it. 'You were right to come here, Anne. This country's hardly been touched since the Gold Rush.'

'Won't it be horribly expensive to bring a film crew here?' she queried.

'If George Lucas can film in the Moroccan desert, I can do it here.'

Despair crept over her. It wasn't going to work. He was already plotting ways and means. She could hardly believe he would consider working in such inhospitable country.

In the film industry, time was indeed money. There was even an expression that described the expensive result of a film running seriously over budget—golden time. Out here, they would be into platinum time, she was sure.

'Why is it so important to be authentic?' she asked, her voice vibrant with disappointment.

'I prefer realism in my films. I hate trying to fool audiences that a corner of Sydney is New York, for instance. I'd rather go to New York and get the real thing.'

'I suppose it's true, then, you did actually climb Mount Everest when you filmed *Heights of Passion*?'

'There was no other way to get the feel for the place that the film demanded,' he told her.

Her eyes flashed fire. 'The film demanded? Don't you mean that *you* demanded? What about the rest of your people? Don't they get tired of being dragged to exotic, dangerous places to get you the results you want? It's a strange way to behave, putting people's lives in danger for the sake of entertainment.'

His eyes locked with hers, the blue depths turning wintry with fury. Muscles worked in his throat and her own went dry as she realised she'd gone too far. 'Have you quite finished?' he asked coldly.

Her hand went to her throat as if to choke off the words she regretted uttering. But it was too late. 'I'm sorry, I didn't mean what I said,' she whispered.

'You meant every word. It's obvious that you have nothing but contempt for the film industry, even though it fed, clothed and educated you.'

It was more or less what her mother had said when Anne complained about the director attempting to molest her. Finding that Tom felt the same left a bitter taste in her mouth. 'You don't understand,' she protested.

'I understand all right. You think, because it comes with degrees and scientific jargon, that the quest for gold is more respectable than what I do. But what difference is there, really? You fuel people's dreams, and so do I.'

Horrified at the anger she had unleashed in him, she took a few faltering steps backwards, coming up against a sapling and clutching it with both hands behind her, as if it was a lifeline. 'I never thought of it that way,' she confessed in a low tone.

'Then maybe it's time you did.'

He spun around and she heard his crashing progress back to camp. She felt drained and defeated. No matter what she did, he was going to make his film here. He had no right to make it sound so noble. How dared he compare her work to his?

At the same time, there came the nagging suspicion that he was right. What was so terrible about helping people to escape from their problems for a while? Then she remembered the producer with his wandering hands and the actor playing the field while his wife waited at home. Tom's aims might be noble, but the reality fell far short.

There was only one solution. Since she couldn't change his mind, she had to leave. She would make the arrangements while Tom was back in Perth assembling his crew. By the time he returned, she would be gone.

The thought of leaving Kalgoorlie tore at her. She had made a life in the goldfields, put down roots for the first time in her life. She would miss Nancy and Greg, and Sam, her boss, and the kids at the drop-in centre. She wouldn't see the results of her fund-raising work. Yet what other choice did she have if she wanted to keep her anonymity?

She decided to say nothing to Tom. He was unlikely to be pleased about her decision, although it had nothing to do with him.

He was stirring stew over the campfire when she joined him. The flickering flames emphasised the craggy angles and planes of his face, making him look more ruggedly handsome than usual. Anne's heart constricted in protest. Reacting to Tom as a man wasn't part of her plans, so why did her body keep betraying her this way?

He looked up and saw her watching him. 'Hungry?'

'A little.'

He ladled stew into a bowl for her and added a chunk of crusty bread. She took it and settled down beside the fire. She sensed Tom's curiosity about her antagonism towards the film industry when it had, indeed, provided her mother's living, so she got in first. 'How long have you been a producer?'

'I started in my teens, working my way up through the ranks. I could have started in my father's company, but I preferred to work my way up.'

'Is your father still in the business?'

She was startled to see a mixture of anger and pain cloud his eyes as he set his plate down. 'My father died eight years ago, as you very well know.'

It must have happened while she was in Queensland, establishing herself as a geologist. Cursing herself for being tactless, she said, 'I'm sorry. I didn't actually know your father, but my mother worked with him several times.'

He fixed her with a hard, uncompromising glare. 'How can you say you never knew my father?'

'Because I didn't.' What was the matter with him? 'We might have met at a studio party, but if we did I don't remember.'

He rose, towering over her, a frightening figure in the gathering darkness. He was really angry now, although why she couldn't guess. His teeth gleamed whitely in the firelight and his eyes flashed molten fire. She didn't want him to look at her so angrily. She wanted... she wanted...

'You don't remember,' he repeated in a dangerously low voice. 'You don't remember the man you and your mother drove to his death?'

CHAPTER FIVE

ANNE'S head swung from side to side until her hair spilled across her face in a heavy curtain. She swept it back impatiently. 'I don't know who you're mixing me up with, but you're wrong. I had nothing to do with your father's death.'

In the firelight, the veins pulsed savagely at each side of Tom's head. His eyes were dark pools of implacable fury. He began to pad around the campsite, apparently to pace off his anger, reminding her of a tiger in a wildlife reserve.

Then he swung around, the flames catching the fire in his eyes. 'I might have known you'd deny it, but you and your mother are jointly to blame for what happened to my father.'

'How can we be?' she protested. 'I didn't even know he was dead until you told me just now.'

His brows drew together into a dark line. 'I must admit, you're quite convincing. If I didn't know better, I'd——'

'I'm convincing because I'm telling the truth,' she cut across him.

'Why should I believe a consummate actress like you?'

A wave of anger engulfed her. 'Stop this! First of all, I'm not any kind of actress. I only made one film, and I was so bad that the film wasn't fit to release. And secondly——'

'What?' Tom froze in mid-step and pivoted around, clearing the campfire in one stride. His hands came under her arms and he hauled her to her feet, his face disturbingly close to hers. His breath was a warm zephyr on her cheeks. 'Say that again,' he insisted.

How could she think straight when he was so close? Yet to escape would mean putting up an undignified struggle. Anne forced herself to remain still. 'Say what again?'

'What was that about your film?'

Her thoughts spun in dizzying circles. What had she said? 'It was a disaster,' she repeated. 'I was so bad that the film was never released, so I *know* what sort of actress I am.'

He eased her to the ground, but kept his punishing hold on her shoulders. 'You're lying. You have to be.'

He wasn't making any sense. 'Why should I be? I saw the rushes myself and they were terrible. That's why the film was never released.'

His fingers bit into the tender skin of her shoulders. Distantly she wondered if she would have bruises there tomorrow. He seemed unaware of the pressure he was exerting as he fought to make sense of what she had told him. 'You knew that Howard Callander was the producer, didn't you?'

'Executive producer,' she corrected him. 'He wasn't the actual producer, but the film was made by your father's company. What does that have to do with anything?'

'Everything. Your mother and my father had an affair years ago, and she used the fact as leverage to make him suppress the picture. She told him it was what you wanted, and she'd tell everyone about their affair if he didn't co-operate.'

Shock made Anne double up in sudden pain, and he caught her, helping her on to a folding chair. 'I can't believe my mother would do such a thing!' she gasped. 'To blackmail your father and say it was my idea...'

'Then it wasn't what you wanted?'

She raised anguished eyes to him. 'Never. The picture was a mistake, but I was the one who made it. If I came out of it looking like a fool, I had no one to blame but myself.'

'How noble of you.'

His sneering comment drew her head up. 'It wasn't noble. The damage was done. I had no choice but to accept it.'

'Only your mother didn't choose to accept it, did she?'

There was no escaping the conclusion that Joanna had gone to Howard Callander and forced him to suppress the film, using their previous relationship as a lever. 'She must have thought she was protecting me,' Anne said, the hopelessness in her voice mirroring her inner despair. How could Joanna do such a thing?

'Joanna was protecting herself, as she always does,' Tom ground out. 'But this time she went too far. My father had a heart condition she didn't know about. Her threat to wreck his marriage by exposing their affair brought on a series of heart attacks. The last one was massive and fatal.'

Anne felt numb with shock. 'I'm so sorry,' she said on a half-sob. 'I didn't know, I swear.'

He could have been carved from granite for all
the response her sympathy evoked. Never had she
seen a human being in such torment. Her stomach
churned as she realised he still hadn't decided
whether or not to believe her.

'Please . . . don't . . . look at me . . . like that,' she
implored. 'I didn't know. You have to believe me.
I didn't know!'

Tears threatened to choke her and she had to
move, to escape from his accusing eyes. She pushed
herself out of the folding chair, which crashed to
the ground behind her. She didn't notice as she
stumbled into the darkness at the rim of the
firelight.

Where she went didn't seem to matter as long as
it was away from Tom. She couldn't stand having
him look at her as if she was a murderer. 'Why,
Mother, why?' she sobbed into the darkness. The
bush answered with silence.

Branches whipped across her face as she pushed
on, tree roots snagging her ankles, until she reached
a clearing and stood with her back against a tree-
trunk, fighting to catch her breath.

She knew that her mother had pulled strings to
have the film withdrawn, but she had never
dreamed that Joanna would go so far. Tom believed her mother was protecting herself, but that
didn't make sense. Unless . . .

Anne's breath caught on a sob as she realised he
was right. Joanna must have been afraid that her
daughter's terrible performance would reflect badly
on her own career. Why else would she take such
drastic measures?

At least Joanna hadn't known about Howard Callander's heart condition. She couldn't be blamed for deliberately causing his death. But did it matter when the outcome was the same?

'Coo-ee! Coo-ee!'

The traditional Australian bush call broke the silence, and Anne tensed, poised to continue her flight into the scrub. Tom was looking for her, but she didn't want to see him or speak to him. How could she face him when it was her fault that he had been robbed of his father?

Although she hadn't known how Joanna intended to have the film suppressed, Anne had to accept some of the blame. If she were a better actress, the film might have been good enough for release. Then her mother wouldn't have been driven to do what she did.

'It's all my fault,' she gasped into the darkness, burying her face in her hands. Why had she agreed to make the wretched film in the first place? She could have refused and worked her way through her degree, as so many other students did. It would have taken longer, perhaps years longer, but she wouldn't be faced with this terrible burden now.

'Anne, where are you?'

Tom was coming closer. She couldn't face him yet, and her heart thudded painfully as she heard him closing in on her. A light bobbed through the bush as he found his way by torchlight.

Suddenly the beam of light invaded her clearing and she made out Tom's bulky shape behind it. She had to get away.

'Anne, wait!' he called.

In desperation, she clawed through the thicket surrounding the clearing and plunged into the tangled scrub. Prickly spinifex tore at her and she thrust it aside, welcoming the small cuts and scratches as penance for the harm she had caused. She couldn't bear the thought that Tom had suffered because of her. His father was dead. What were a few cuts and scratches by comparison?

Without warning, her foot caught in a tree root and her boot was almost wrenched off by the force of the impact as she crashed to the ground. Fiery pain stabbed at her ankle and radiated up her calf. She clutched at it, moaning in anger and frustration.

A string of explicit curses tore the air as a beam of light caught and held her, then Tom dropped down beside her. Well might he curse her, she thought, after what she had done to him.

But his anger was directed at the tangle of roots imprisoning her ankle. 'Damned things, they're enough to break anybody's neck.'

'I'm sorry—I was a clumsy fool,' she said, gritting her teeth against the pain. In all the years she had worked alone in the outback, this was the first time she'd ever injured herself. Why did it have to happen now, with Tom?

The fingers probing her ankles were surprisingly gentle. 'I'm the one who should apologise. I was so sure you were behind your mother's actions that it never occurred to me you might not know what she'd done.'

'Then you believe me?'

'How can I not? *Nobody's* that good an actor.'

Sweet relief flooded through her as she said emphatically, 'Especially not me.'

He gave her a searching look but didn't argue as he completed his examination of her ankle. 'It doesn't feel too serious. I can move my toes,' she told him, then bit her lip as the movement caused a wave of pain.

He frowned. 'It looks like a sprain, but you won't be bushwalking for a few days.' He slid a hand under her knees and the other around her shoulders, scooping her into his arms.

She didn't know which shock was greater, hurting her ankle or finding herself in his arms. 'This is crazy. I can hop if you help me,' she insisted.

'You might do more damage. Relax. You weigh almost nothing.'

He carried her as if she did, striding through the tangled underbrush towards the lights of their camp with the surefootedness of a bushman. She was the one who belonged out here, yet he claimed it as his own merely by the way he walked across the land.

'I'm supposed to be leading you,' she protested.

Tom gave a throaty chuckle that sent goosebumps surging up her neck. 'You really think so?'

Indignation flooded through her. 'Of course I do. It was my idea to bring you to this no-man's-land so that you...you....' Her voice tailed off as she fell headlong into his trap.

'So that I'd be put off the idea of making a film here,' he finished for her. 'Nice try, sweetheart, but it had no hope of working. I did my homework before I came to Kalgoorlie. If the proposition had been uneconomic, I wouldn't have wasted my time.'

So her plan had been doomed to failure from the beginning. She might as well have stuck to the main roads and saved herself the punishing ride as well as this stupid injury. Holding back tears became a mighty effort, and a stifled sob managed to escape.

'Is the leg hurting, or is it just your pride?'

He was taking her attempt at deception so well that there was no point in trying to brazen it out. 'A bit of both, I suppose,' she admitted.

'Then let it be a lesson to you.'

It was said with such compassion that she knew he would never wish an injury on her, no matter what the provocation. She began to feel even more weepy, angrily blaming it on self-pity, before she realised it was more likely to be the shock of the fall. She shivered and her teeth began to chatter.

In a haze of pain and chills, she felt his lips brush her hairline. 'Take it easy, sweetheart, we're almost there,' he said gently.

The kiss and the endearment meant nothing, she reminded herself. He was only doing what anyone would have done.

Except that anyone wouldn't have triggered such a disturbing variety of sensations as those which assailed her in his arms. Crushed against his chest, her breasts were gently massaged until her nipples tautened, sending urgent messages of need to her startled brain.

His hold was unwavering, the fingers curving around her knees and back with an intimacy she knew she ought to resist, but couldn't summon the strength. Instead, her hands tightened around the firm column of his neck and she buried her face against his shirt.

When they reached the camp, he pushed aside the tent flap with his shoulder and ducked under the low doorway to set her down on top of his sleeping-bag.

Anne struggled upright. 'This is your bed. I can't——'

He pushed her firmly down again. 'For once, you'll do as you're told.'

It was a welcome change to let someone else take charge, she found, surprised at herself. With her mother working so much of the time, she had become self-reliant almost from the time of her father's death. It was no easy task to let someone else make decisions for her, but it felt amazingly good.

Tom foraged through the portable refrigerator and came up with a package of ice. 'This may hurt,' he warned as he eased her boot off.

'There's no "may" about it,' she said through gritted teeth. 'Of all the stupid, amateurish things to do...'

He looked up from applying the ice to her rapidly swelling ankle. 'It was a fairly normal reaction to being accused of something you didn't do.'

Curiosity overcame her pain. 'What made you decide to believe me?'

'I couldn't imagine you faking such a strong re-action. It was obvious you hadn't known anything about Dad's death until I told you.'

Her hand drifted to his hair, which was on a level with her shoulder, but she let it drop before touching him. 'I am sorry about your father,' she said softly.

'I know. I've had time to get used to being without him, but there are times when I want to talk over some aspect of the business, or some new idea. Then there's this hollow feeling as I remember that he isn't there.'

'My dad died when I was ten,' she told him. 'You'd think I'd be over it by now, but there are times when I feel the same way,' she confessed.

'Was he in the film business too?'

She shook her head, easing her foot around so the ice could soothe the damaged joint. 'No, he was a lawyer. He met my mother when a client invested in one of her films.'

'So what happened?'

'A drunk driver ran into his car when he was coming home to us one night.'

Tom gave a heartfelt sigh. 'Hell! What a waste.'

'It was.' She was about to add that things might have been different for their family if her father had lived, but it seemed like a betrayal of her mother to admit it, even to Tom. Maybe especially to Tom. The last thing she wanted was his pity.

He stood up, hefting the ice pack in one hand. 'I think the swelling's stabilised now. I'll strap up the joint, then you can get some sleep.'

She didn't want to sleep. More than anything, she wanted to prolong the wonderful sense of intimacy which the night and her injury had established. In daylight, it would all be different. She felt a need to keep him by her side for as long as possible.

'Why did you let me bring you here if you knew what I was up to?' she asked.

Tom turned back, folding his arms across his chest. In the harsh fluorescent light, his eyes were dark pools. 'I wanted to see how far you'd take this plan of yours.'

'Not much further.' She rubbed the back of her head where it had bumped repeatedly against the roof of the car. 'I'd already started regretting it.'

'Besides, I was enjoying myself,' he said, and this time she glimpsed a spark of amusement in the dark depths.

'You were?'

'Sure. I've seen a lot of the goldfields first hand and ventured into country which has hardly changed since the Gold Rush. My notebook is bulging with ideas. I can hardly complain.'

He came back with the first-aid kit and took out an elastic bandage, winding it expertly around her ankle joint until it was immobilised. 'How does it feel now?'

'Much better, thanks.'

'I'm glad. I'd hate to have to try and drive out of here in the dark.'

Anne was amazed he'd even consider such a thing, and hastily suppressed the elation that flooded through her. His willingness to risk the drive had nothing to do with her as a person, only as a fellow human being who was injured and needed his help. He'd have done the same for anyone.

Nevertheless, she felt comforted by the thought as she turned her face into his sleeping-bag, breathing in the musky scent of him captured by the thickly padded fabric.

She was almost asleep when something warm and scratchy was draped over her. 'Th-thanks,' she said through chattering teeth, gathering the blanket tightly around herself.

'It's the shock of the fall catching up with you,' Tom diagnosed. 'I'll get you another blanket.'

'No, please. Stay here a while.'

'If you like.'

His curt tone told her she was probably imposing, but she needed the warmth of his presence more than she needed another blanket. Something electric jolted through her as he took both of her hands in his, chafing them to stimulate the circulation. When her hands were warm, he tucked them inside his shirt to keep them that way and started massaging her shoulders.

Imprisoned against his chest, her hands tangled in his ample chest hair. His body heat radiated along her arms and all through her body as his touch on her shoulders made her want to arch her back and purr like a kitten. Her fingers strayed along either side of his rib cage and her thumbs began a subtle rotating pressure, until she heard his breathing quicken.

Without warning, his hands dipped to the small of her back and he pulled her against him. When he bent his head, she gave a small mew that was half protest, half invitation, but her lips parted and the invitation won. He kissed her.

All thoughts of the pain in her ankle fled in the face of the exquisite pleasure his kiss invoked. The last time he had kissed her, he had been responding to her defiant challenge, but this time was something entirely different. There was tenderness in the way his mouth moved over hers, and gentleness in the seeking movements of his tongue, as he explored the moist cavern of her mouth. She wanted to laugh and cry with the bitter-sweet pleasure of it.

But when his fingers went to the buttons of her shirt and started flicking them open, she came to her senses. 'No, I...this isn't...I don't...' she began.

Tom regarded her with mild amusement. 'You don't what?'

'I don't want this,' she managed to get out.

He withdrew her hands from his shirt and kissed the tips of her fingers, sending erotic sensations shooting down her arms. 'I get a different message.'

'I know, and I'm sorry, but...' Sanity was returning with a rush. How could she let herself forget who and what he was? Now she knew why he had sought her out, she had even more reason to keep a safe distance.

He studied her panicky expression. 'What is it, Anne?'

'I told you I don't believe in casting couches.'

She had hurt him, she saw from the sudden darkening of his eyes and the frown that lined his tanned forehead. 'Is that what you think this is?' he demanded.

'What else can it be? We hardly know each other.'

'A situation which can be easily remedied,' he assured her. 'Assuming you want to remedy it?'

He was leaving the next step up to her. Panic flared through her. She didn't want to start something which would be over as soon as his film was finished, if it even lasted that long.

Yet how could she say she didn't want to see him again when every fibre of her being cried out for his touch? Perhaps the best way to rid herself of the...obsession was the only word for it, was to see him again in her normal surroundings. Perhaps then she could be as coolly sensible as she knew she should be.

'Yes,' she said on a sigh.

'Then so be it.'

He tucked her hands underneath the blanket and pulled it up to her chin. She felt like a child being tucked up in bed.

But there was nothing childlike about the longing that kept her awake for hours after he had climbed the ladder to the car-top bunk.

She must be crazy even thinking about seeing him again. He might deny the reality of the casting couch, but she had experienced it for herself.

Tom's different, a small voice inside her insisted. She had no proof of it. In fact, the speed with which he had overcome her resistance suggested he was just like the others in his profession.

Apples on a tree, she murmured to herself, tossing and turning as her ankle pained her. Or was it the pain in her heart for which there was no easy treatment?

The tantalising aroma of coffee finally intruded on her restless dreams. She yawned and stretched, wondering when she had managed to fall asleep.

Tom's face appeared at the tent flap and he carried a steaming mug of coffee. 'Ready for this?' he asked.

She grimaced. 'I should switch to decaffeinated, but I love my heart-starter in the mornings.'

'Me too.' He placed the cup on a suitcase within easy reach of her bunk. 'How's the ankle this morning?'

She flexed it as fully as the bandage allowed. 'The swelling's gone down and the pain is almost gone,' she announced.

'Then you should be able to manage the trip back to Kalgoorlie today.'

Disappointment lanced through her. 'Have you finished your research already?' she queried.

'No, but I want a doctor to take a look at your ankle.'

Anne felt like a child deprived of a promised treat. 'There's no need—I'll be fine.'

'Nevertheless, we're starting back after breakfast.' Tom gave her a stern look as she opened her mouth to protest, then shut it again. 'Good. I was beginning to think you argued for the sake of it.'

Only with him, she thought. With everyone else, she was coolly professional, a team player who could follow orders without question. Tom was the only one who could throw her off balance with a simple command. As she sipped her coffee, she avoided looking too closely at why it should be so.

Overruling her protestations, he made her sit on a tree stump and watch while he broke camp and repacked the four-wheel-drive.

'I feel useless sitting here,' she complained as he lashed the car-top tent back into place.

'Then make yourself useful. Talk to me,' he commanded over his shoulder.

'What about?'

'You, for starters. Did you know you talked in your sleep last night?'

Her startled gaze flickered to his face. 'I did? What about?'

'You seemed to be running away from someone and you didn't want him to touch you. What was that all about?'

Her mention of the casting couch last night must have triggered her old nightmare about the producer who had tried to molest her during her first audition. The dream had recurred often until she reached her twenties. She hadn't had it for ages. Was it some sort of omen to beware of getting involved with Tom?

'I was probably dreaming about something unpleasant which happened to me years ago,' she said lightly.

Tom wasn't deceived. 'Was it the reason why you turned your back on the film industry?'

Was he reading her mind now? 'It was part of the reason,' she said carefully.

Tom finished securing the tent and dusted off his hands. 'I suspect it was a big part. Maybe you'll trust me with the story when we get to know each other better.'

So he hadn't forgotten last night's promise. 'Look, maybe it isn't such a good idea for us to see each other again,' Anne began.

Touching a hand under her chin, he tilted her face up to his. 'I want to see you again, Anne. If you don't agree, I'm not in the habit of forcing myself on any woman. But I think I deserve an explanation.'

She wasn't up to explaining right now. It was easier to stand by their agreement. He looked satisfied when she said so. 'That's more like it,' he said.

It was as if the decision was out of her hands, she realised as he drove carefully back to the main road. Fate seemed to be sweeping her along in Tom's direction.

It was easier to go along than to fight, she told herself, trying to ignore the traitorous thought that she *wanted* to be swept away. For the first time since she had come to Kalgoorlie, she felt vibrantly alive, as if she had awakened from a long sleep.

It had to be the lure of forbidden fruit, she told herself. Tom Callander was bad for her in every way. He was precisely the sort of man she had come to the goldfields to avoid.

So why did she feel as if a whole troupe of butterflies was performing in her stomach? It couldn't be because, the next time she saw him, it wouldn't be strictly business, could it?

CHAPTER SIX

FOR the hundredth time that evening, Anne's eyes strayed to the clock. It must be broken. The hands hadn't moved more than a quarter of an hour since last she looked at them.

A reluctant smile broke over her face. The clock wasn't to blame. It was her own ambivalence about seeing Tom again. She had kept her promise and had agreed to have dinner with him at the new French restaurant tonight. He was due to arrive at any moment. But was she doing the right thing?

Since they returned to Kalgoorlie a week ago, he had telephoned her every day to see how her ankle was mending. He hadn't mentioned his father again, and she still hadn't made up her mind what to do about his accusation that her mother had hastened his father's death. She would have to talk to Joanna, she supposed, but the damage was done. But Joanna could be stopped from acting in Anne's name in future.

Luckily, the damage to her ankle wasn't serious, as the company doctor had assured her when Tom took her to his surgery. Staying off her feet, which was the doctor's prescription, had been harder than the initial injury, although Sam had encouraged her to take all the time off she needed.

Now her ankle had mended sufficiently to allow her to wear her black patent evening shoes. It would have been dreadful to go out wearing a smart black dinner dress and jogging shoes, which were all she could wear for the first few days.

What had made her so fashion-conscious all of a sudden? What she wore on her feet hadn't seemed to matter until Tom came along.

There she had it. Until Tom.

Suddenly her life was divisible into before Tom and after he came into her life. What did it mean? She was almost afraid to find out.

A knock on the door interrupted her reverie, and she opened it to find Tom almost hidden behind an enormous bouquet of roses.

Her hope that she could treat this as another business meeting wasn't going to work, she saw now. She buried her face in the fragrant mass. 'Roses in the outback? They must have cost you a fortune.'

He shook his head. 'Wrong response.'

He looked annoyed, and she felt guilty for being so ungracious. 'Thank you. They're lovely.'

Tom gave a satisfied nod. 'Much better.'

He followed her to her tiny kitchenette, where she found a vase for the flowers. 'I haven't had much practice at this sort of thing,' she said by way of further apology.

He took in the low cut of her dress. The simplicity of the wrap-around design was set off by a series of tiny crystal buttons at the front which emphasised her small waist and high, full breasts. 'Frankly, I find it hard to believe,' he told her.

Her nervous laugh punctuated the silence that followed. 'Thanks, but it's true. I bought this dress for a mining industry dinner.'

'Then it's time it found its true vocation.'

Anne felt her skin reddening. First flowers, now compliments. When Tom had invited her to dinner, she hadn't expected such gallantry. It threw her completely off balance. She was glad when another knock on the door provided a diversion.

It was Nancy. She looked flustered as she came into the living-room. 'I'm glad I caught you in. Greg just telephoned to say he'll be out in the field longer than he planned—he was supposed to be back today. Jenny's coming down with a cold, so I can't take her with me, and I simply must go tonight.'

Anne was confused by the flood of details. 'Go where?'

'The fashion show I arranged for the drop-in centre. I'm the compère, so I can't ask someone else to take over at such short notice.' Nancy gave Anne a look of appeal. 'Could you possibly babysit for me tonight?'

Nancy was so agitated that she hadn't noticed what Anne was wearing, she realised. She hated to let her friend down, but there was Tom to consider too. 'Oh, Nancy, I——'

'We'll be glad to help out,' said Tom, stepping out from behind the kitchen divider.

Nancy's eyes widened. 'Mr Callander! I didn't know you were here.' Belatedly, she noticed Anne's evening clothes. 'You two have a date, don't you?'

'We can still have a date at your place,' Tom put in.

'But you're all dressed up. I can't expect you to...'

'You don't have to. We're volunteering.' His gaze went to Anne and he nodded imperceptibly. 'Aren't we, Anne?'

'It looks like it,' she said, nonplussed. She would gladly have given up her evening out to help her friend, but she was astonished that Tom wanted to.

Nancy's arguments faded away on an outpouring of breath. 'I feel terrible about this, but I have to accept. You two are angels sent from heaven.'

'There's no need to go overboard. Just lead us to your offspring and brief us on any details, then you can be on your way.'

Nancy and Greg lived in a two-bedroomed bungalow across the road from Anne's building. The children were already in bed when they arrived, although both were wide awake and pleased to see Anne. They were a little shy around Tom, but he put them at ease with a skill that amazed both women.

'This isn't his first time at babysitting,' Nancy whispered to Anne, while Tom squatted between the single beds, talking to the children.

Anne felt a surge of apprehension. Was he divorced or, worse, still married with children of his own? She had a vision of the married actor dating the young starlet at her mother's party. Was Tom playing similar games with her?

When they knew where to contact Nancy if she was needed, and what medication to give Jenny if her cold worsened, Tom shooed Nancy towards the door. 'Go, or you'll be late for your fashion parade,' he ordered.

Nancy's hands fluttered anxiously. 'If it wasn't a fund-raiser...'

'Stop apologising! We'll be fine.'

Still Nancy wavered. 'If you want some food...'

'I'll telephone the restaurant and have them send something over,' he said firmly. 'Goodnight, Nancy.'

'Well, goodnight, and...and thanks.'

They finally persuaded her to leave, and Anne dropped on to the couch, smiling broadly. 'I thought she'd never stop thanking us and go to her function.'

'You don't mind spending the evening here?'

'No, but I'm surprised you're so keen.'

He joined her on the couch, stretching an arm comfortably along the back so his hand nearly touched her shoulder. 'I'm an old hand at this,' he assured her.

Tension built up inside her. Was he about to confirm her worst suspicions? 'So I gathered. Is it because you have children of your own?'

Something in her voice alerted him and he cupped her chin, tilting her head so she faced him. 'Is that what you think?'

She didn't want to meet his searching gaze, but he left her no choice. 'You never mentioned a wife,' she said, dropping sooty lashes over her stinging eyes.

'Mainly because I've never had one. Nor do I have a trail of children scattered around the place.'

'But you said——'

'I said I'm an old hand at babysitting,' he cut in. His voice was vibrant with suppressed laughter. 'Both my parents were film-makers, so I practically brought up my twin sisters. They're ten years younger than me, so I was usually left in charge.'

Relief made her sag slightly in his grasp. 'I see.'

His bent knuckles caressed the side of her face. 'So you can stop looking so worried.' He grew more serious. 'I may have what used to be called a reputation, but I've done nothing I wasn't legally and morally entitled to do.'

It was hard to concentrate with his touch playing havoc with her senses. 'I know,' she whispered. She had fashioned her own standards in spite of her upbringing. There was no reason why Tom shouldn't have done the same.

He didn't withdraw his hand, and the air between them became electric. She wanted to turn her face and bury it in his palm, to slide across the couch until their bodies were touching and . . .

'Anne, Jenny's got my torch, and she won't give it back. Make her give it back!'

The little boy's high-pitched appeal from the children's bedroom shattered the moment. Reluctantly, Anne pushed herself to her feet. 'I'll go and referee.'

Tom's expression was tinged with regret. Had he understood her temptation to move into his arms, perhaps shared the power of her desires? 'I'll call the restaurant about our dinner, then I'll read the little monsters a story,' he said.

She smiled wryly. 'I hope you know what you're getting into.'

With the telephone in hand, he favoured her with a dark look. 'I could say the same to you.'

The promise of a story from Tom was enough to quieten the children. They were still a little awed by him, and readily settled down to hear a favourite about green eggs and ham.

Watching from the doorway, Anne discovered that Tom knew the rhyming story by heart. It was so at odds with her earlier impressions of him that a lump rose in her throat. She tiptoed back into the living-room.

While she waited, a courier arrived with their food. Fragrant aromas wafted from several insulated containers, and she hunted up cutlery and dinnerware from Nancy's kitchen. Everything was ready when Tom emerged from the children's room.

'They're asleep,' he mouthed, putting the book down. He sniffed the air appreciatively. 'Smells wonderful.'

'How on earth did you get them to deliver Oysters Tzarina and Beef Wellington?' she asked.

His mock frown made her laugh. 'You mean they forgot the crêpes Suzette?'

'No, they didn't forget a thing. There's even an ice bucket for the champagne—which was extravagant of you, by the way.'

He shook his head, laughing. 'Still the wrong response. When will you get it right?'

Her laughter mingled with his. 'Thank you, Tom. This is a lovely treat.'

'Much better.' He pulled a chair out for her and settled a napkin across her knees with a flourish. 'It's exactly the meal we would have had if we'd gone to the restaurant.'

'Except that this is much nicer,' Anne said without thinking.

He took a seat opposite her. 'You're right, it is. Because we have it all to ourselves.'

'For as long as our charges remain asleep,' she reminded him.

Tom poured the champagne and raised his glass. 'Then let's drink to sound sleep for little people.'

Her glass touched his lightly. 'My sentiments exactly.'

After the meal, she could hardly recall what they had talked about. Tom quizzed her about her work, showing an interest she could have sworn was genuine. Then he told her more about the Herbert Hoover film and his plans for the new studio complex. They also discussed the drop-in centre, and he contributed some good ideas for raising more money towards the cost.

But it was as if only half her mind was on the conversation. The other half was preoccupied with how eloquently his long-fingered hands moved when he talked. They could have been a conductor's hands, as they stabbed the air to make a point.

Then there was his hair, which had a metallic gleam in the lamplight. The dark strands at each temple gave him a devilish air. She felt a compelling urge to touch them, to see what the different coloured strands felt like.

'Why do I have the feeling you aren't listening?' he asked suddenly, capturing her full attention.

'Because I wasn't,' she confessed. 'Sorry, my mind was wandering. What did you say?'

His mouth moved over the rim of his wine glass and he savoured a few drops before he answered. 'Maybe it's wandering in the same direction as mine.'

It couldn't be. She wasn't ready for that yet. 'You said something about having the première of your new film in Kalgoorlie,' she prompted through dry lips. Her tongue darted out to moisten them and she saw his quick intake of breath.

'Was that what I said? The première could raise money for your drop-in centre. What do you think?'

'I think...I think...' Oh, lord, she knew what she thought, and it had nothing to do with the youth centre. A montage of images flashed through her mind: Tom kissing her outside her door; cradling her against his chest as he carried her back to camp; gently bathing and binding her ankle, his fingers so strong yet careful of her pain.

'What are you thinking about?' he asked.

She gave him a startled look. Had her tender thoughts strayed on to her face? 'I...it must be the wine,' she defended herself.

His gaze went to the bottle, which was still more than half full. Without discussing it, they hadn't drunk more than a glass each, mindful of their charges in the next room.

Anne's chin dropped on to her hand and she looked at him from under lowered lashes. 'Then what do I blame this on?'

He seemed to know instinctively what she meant, and shrugged. 'Why look for reasons? Isn't it enough just to feel?'

'It depends on the feeling.' What had happened to her voice? It wasn't usually so deep and vibrant. Tom's presence seemed to strip away her defences until none was left. Where was her wariness now? Some time during the evening it had been transmuted into something she hardly dared recognise, a hunger for his nearness, for his touch.

She forced herself to remember what she had read about him in the gossip columns. He seldom lacked female company, she knew, and the smooth way he'd handled this evening spoke of long practice. None of it helped, somehow.

As if in a dream, she saw him leave his seat and come around to her side of the table. His touch on her bare arms was electric as he urged her to her feet. Then she was in his arms, not resisting but moulding herself against him with unseemly eagerness, as if this was where she belonged.

'That's it, sweetheart, just feel,' he murmured, his lips moving seductively against her hairline.

Under the constricting fabric of her dress, her breasts felt tight and hot, as she was crushed against him. She had to resist the urge to tear the dress off, then start on his shirt, until no physical barriers remained between them.

The idea both shocked and fascinated her, and her mind whirled as his mouth sought hers. His hunger more than matched her own, and the possessiveness of his kiss almost took her breath away.

She had been kissed before, but it was hard to equate those experiences with the tumult of sensations Tom ignited inside her. At first tender, then more insistent, he urged her lips apart until she was feeding off him in a way which would have shocked her not long ago.

She went limp in his arms, aligning her aching body to his hard contours. Excitement rippled through her as his arousal became tantalisingly apparent. Power went to her head like a drug. It wasn't all one-sided. She had made him want her too. He shared the driving need to be one that tormented her.

Her heart raced as he deepened the kiss. His hands were hot on her back and neck until she felt as if she would break in two with the power of his embrace. Her hands slid along the column of his neck and she twined her fingers in his hair.

At last she could touch the silky strands of darker hair at his temples. Was it her imagination, or were they coarser than the burnished gold of the rest of his hair? Her fingers tangled in them and she nipped his lower lip between her teeth in a frenzy of need and anticipation.

They were going to make love, and she wanted it more than she had ever wanted anything. A kiss, an embrace, however wonderful, were but overtures to the symphony she longed to share with Tom.

What had happened to the detached, scientific Anne Fleming? It was almost as if Deanne, her alter ego, had swept aside the professional veneer, insisting on her right to exist.

'No!'

Her fierce denial, meant for herself more than for Tom, caused him to draw back, his dark eyes fixed on her in puzzlement. 'What is it? Did I hurt you?' he demanded.

How could she tell him of her sudden fear that this was how Deanne might behave? Not Anne, never Anne. She knew only too well that there was no permanence in Tom's world. To him, living for today was an acceptable, even desirable way to behave. But not to her.

'I just can't, that's all,' she said, appalled by the prim sound of her own voice, but unable to stop herself.

'Are you worried about the children waking up?'

She clutched at the excuse as a lifeline. 'Yes, that's it—the children.'

He thrust a hand through his hair in frustration. 'You're right, of course. But we can't let it end here—you know that, don't you?'

'Maybe it's better if we do,' she whispered.

He shook his head. 'Better for whom? Certainly not me and, I suspect, not you either. You want me, Anne. And I want you. I agree it isn't the right time or place, but there'll be other times and places. You should know by now that I don't give up easily.'

Part of her rejoiced in the reminder, but another part wanted him to give up on her. It would be easier than trying to give up on him, she thought as despair flooded through her. If he walked away, she wouldn't have to make the choice, she accepted wearily. It had gone way past logic and common sense. She had never expected to feel such a compelling need for a man who was wrong for her in every way.

It was almost a relief when Jenny woke up complaining about her cold, so Anne could give her attention to the child for the rest of the evening.

All the same, her heart raced and her pulses pounded when Tom walked her back to her front door. They weren't touching, but awareness of his presence crackled through her like electricity. At her door, his mouth hovered close to her and she was torn between wishing he would kiss her and hoping he wouldn't. 'Next time we'll have a real date with no little distractions,' he promised.

He couldn't know how she blessed those little distractions for saving her from herself. 'It's been a lovely evening, all the same,' she said formally.

He propped an arm against the doorframe, effectively imprisoning her within the circle of his body. 'They'll get better, much better,' he vowed, his eyes warm as they roved over her in the silvery moonlight.

She should end this now, she knew, but, in spite of everything, she wanted to spend another evening with him. Playing with fire it might be, but the flames attracted her as surely as if she had been a moth, driven by her biological imperatives.

'I'd like that,' she heard herself say.

'Right response,' he murmured. 'For a moment, I thought I was going to have to convince you.'

It was herself she should convince that this was madness. What would happen when he finished his film and it was time to return to his studio complex near Perth? He was hardly likely to move to Kalgoorlie to be with her.

Back in Perth, he would have his pick of desirable women. His power as a producer was a natural aphrodisiac—not that he would care. He was such a charismatic man that he could have been a street sweeper and women would have flocked to him. Like her, she thought unhappily. She knew all the hazards, yet she was behaving like the worst sort of groupie. There didn't seem to be any way to stop herself.

'I'll see you tomorrow evening, then,' she said softly as the door yielded to her touch.

'I doubt if I can wait that long,' he murmured, his fingers tracing a fine line along her jaw. It ended at the corner of her mouth and she pressed a kiss to his fingertip. His breathing quickened. 'Have breakfast with me tomorrow in the company dining-room?'

It was too soon and not soon enough. 'Yes, please,' she said. 'I'm going in to see Sam about my next assignment in any case.'

A frown etched his forehead. 'Your current assignment isn't finished yet.'

'But I thought, after the field trip...'

'Then you thought wrong. I need some help interpreting the photos I took.'

'But Sam...' she began.

'Sam assigned you to me for as long as I need you.'

She was fairly sure Sam hadn't meant her to continue working with Tom once they had found his locations for his film. The company needed her as a geologist, out in the field. Yet the prospect of working with Tom for a little while longer was undeniably appealing. 'I'll have to discuss it with Sam,' she said diffidently.

'You do that, then plan on working with me for at least the rest of the month.'

His arrogance was unbelievable, assuming she would even consider working with him for so long. The fact that he was right hardly mattered. He hadn't taken her wishes into account at all. 'We'll see,' she said tautly.

His dark eyes held her captive. 'We'll see that I'm right,' he amended. Then he clasped her shoulders and planted a feather-light kiss on her

forehead like a benediction. 'Until breakfast tomorrow, then. Sleep well.'

The imprint of his lips remained on her forehead
long after her strode off into the night. Anne
watched him until he was swallowed up by the
darkness, then turned dreamily and went inside.

With a cup of herb tea in hand, she curled up in
an armchair and replayed every moment of the
evening. When she got to the moment when Tom
took her in his arms, a wave of heat swept over her.
Would he have made love to her if it hadn't been
for the children sleeping in the next room? Was it
what she wanted?

Even as her mind said no, her body argued yes.
Every one of his touches left her aching for more.
She felt hollow inside, wanting his possession more
than she had ever wanted anything.

No amount of arguing with herself would change
the feeling, she knew. Maybe they should make
love. Wanting was said to be better than having. If
it was true, then this feeling should go away once
she gave in to it.

Of course, there was also the risk that once she
knew the sweetness of his possession no other man
would be able to satisfy her ever again. With
shocking clarity, she recognised this as the greater
likelihood.

In growing despair, she drained her cup and got
ready for bed. For the first time, her bachelor
quarters seemed cold and lonely. For a long time
she lay awake wondering what Tom was doing. Was
he thinking of her? The thought sent her lips
curving into a smile as she finally drifted off to
sleep.

Next morning she was up bright and early, telling herself that her blithe mood had nothing to do with seeing Tom again. There was bound to be gossip when they were seen together in the dining-room, but it didn't seem to matter. Nothing mattered any more except the time she spent in his company.

She was halfway through her coffee when the knock came, and her heart did a small somersault of joy, before she schooled herself to behave. She was acting like a lovesick teenager.

The thought brought her up short, her hand on the doorknob. Lovesick? Was it possible? Could she have been such a fool as to fall in love with Tom? A leaden feeling accompanied the thought, quenching her euphoria. You couldn't fall in love with someone against your will, could you?

But it could happen against your better judgement, her inner voice responded. And what was love, if not the dizzying variety of sensations she'd experienced from the day he entered her life?

Oh, God, it made no sense at all, but she *was* in love with him. She knew it as well as she knew her way around the goldfields. When and how it had happened really didn't matter. What mattered was what she was going to do about it.

Her caller knocked again more impatiently and she swung the door open. 'Mother!' she gasped in astonishment. 'What on earth are you doing in Kalgoorlie?'

'Visiting my daughter,' answered Joanna as if it were the most natural thing in the world. 'Aren't you going to invite me in?'

'Of course—come in.' Anne peered around the door as if expecting more surprises, but there was none, and she followed Joanna inside.

Her mother was still a dazzlingly attractive woman, with vivid ash-blonde hair, translucent skin and a figure which was the envy of women half her age. She was dressed for her idea of the country, in designer jeans and a silk shirt which no doubt cost more in dry-cleaning than most of Anne's clothes cost to buy.

Violet shadows rimmed her mother's lustrous brown eyes, Anne noticed as they kissed cheeks. 'It's so good to see you, Dee. How are you, darling?'

A cloud of Joy perfume enveloped Anne. 'I'm fine, but stunned. Why didn't you let me know you were coming? I'd have met you at the airport.'

'It was a spur-of-the-moment decision. I'm not working at present, so it seemed a good time to pay a call.'

'You do look tired. Have you been working hard?' Anne asked.

Joanna bit her full lower lip. 'A bit, but I'll bounce back. I always do, don't I?' Her questioning gaze rested on Anne.

'Of course,' she supplied the expected reassurance. 'Where are you staying, and for how long?'

Joanna named a nearby hotel. 'I haven't decided for how long, but we'll make the most of it, won't we?'

Anne clasped her hands together. 'I can't believe you're actually here. You always vowed you'd never come.'

'That was before . . . never mind, I'm here, aren't I?'

Before what? Anne wanted to ask, but she knew Joanna would tell her when she was ready. Some disastrous love affair had probably driven her here. No doubt Anne would hear all the details in due course.

Joanna consulted her watch. 'I came early to shanghai you for breakfast at my hotel, in case you have to work today.'

'I'm sorry, I can't.' The shock of her mother's arrival had swept her date with Tom from her mind. What would he say when he found Joanna Flame here, knowing what she had done to his father?

'Nonsense. You can't start work this early, not after I came all this way to see you.'

After how many years? Anne thought mutinously, then quelled the thought. Joanna was still her mother and she loved her, in spite of everything. 'I'm not working, I'm having breakfast with a . . . a business associate,' she improvised. It was true, after all.

'Then I'll join you both. It will be good for your business,' said Joanna, undeterred. She took it for granted that her star status would benefit Anne's work, whatever it might be.

'I don't think it's a good idea,' Anne began. 'Why don't I come to your hotel afterwards and we can have a good talk?'

'All right, if it's what you want.'

They were almost at the door when Anne's luck ran out and there was a commanding knock.

Interest flickered in Joanna's eyes. 'Is that your business associate?' she queried.

'Very likely,' Anne said on a sigh, and opened the door. 'I believe you two already know each other.'

CHAPTER SEVEN

Tom's initial surprise turned to cool appraisal. 'Hello, Joanna. I didn't expect to find you here.'

Joanna's eyebrows flickered upwards. 'You could sound a little more pleased about it, darling.'

'I'm never pleased to see you, and you're well aware of the reason,' he said flatly.

The star's alarmed gaze went to Anne. 'We needn't involve Dee in our affairs, surely?'

Sick of being ignored, Anne stepped between them. 'My name isn't Dee, Mother, and Tom has told me everything.'

The colour drained from Joanna's face and she whirled on Tom. 'How could you?' she cried.

'I had a right to know, Mother. I was involved, after all.'

She had never seen her mother look so shocked. She seemed to shrink into herself, and the sight frightened Anne until she remembered what a superb actress Joanna was. The star's expression softened as she looked at Anne. 'I did it for you, darling. You must believe me.'

'Why should she believe you?' Tom demanded. 'Even now, she still doesn't know the whole story.'

Panic flared through Anne. What more could there possibly be? 'I know enough,' she said, tears threading her voice. 'And I wish to God I could do something to make amends, but it's too late.'

Her mother looked thoughtful. 'Maybe it isn't.'

Suspicion seized Anne. 'What do you mean?'

But her mother's glance went to Tom. 'Have you asked her yet?'

'Asked me what?' They were up to something, and Anne had a horrible suspicion that it involved her. When Tom remained silent, she gripped his arm. 'What have you two cooked up between you?'

'We haven't cooked anything up, as you put it. Your mother has about as much tact as a bull elephant at a dinner party.'

'Sticks and stones, sticks and stones,' Joanna said airily. 'It's just as well I came along, or you'd never have got around to it.'

'I planned to be a little more diplomatic.'

Anne pressed her palms to the sides of her head. 'Will one of you please tell me what's going on?'

'Tom has the most marvellous part for you in his film,' Joanna confided as if she was the bearer of great news.

Anne's stomach churned. A part for her in his film? They couldn't mean it. Her mother was mistaken. She shook her head determinedly. 'Oh, no— no, you couldn't, Tom, not that.'

'It shouldn't be a surprise to you. I said all along you're perfect for the part of Katie Dooley, the young lover.'

The scene at Niagara Dam! He had been auditioning her for the part even then. 'You didn't say you wanted me to play her,' she said accusingly.

He glared at Joanna. 'I wanted to tell you in my own way and time.'

Forgetting that her mother was there, Anne swung around. 'When did you plan to bring it up? When we were in bed together?'

'It wasn't like that,' he said quietly.

Wasn't it? Was he going to pretend that his kisses were genuine, that he really wanted to make love to her? He was probably thanking his lucky stars for Nancy and her babysitting assignment last night. It had saved him from having to take his act any further, pretending he cared for her when he was really using her to get what he wanted all along.

'It doesn't matter now,' she said in a voice so low that it was barely audible. The scales had well and truly fallen from her eyes. He couldn't talk his way around her any more. 'I'm not doing the film, so you may as well save your breath.'

Joanna looked shocked. 'Whyever not, dear? It's a wonderful part, and the publicity will be fantastic.'

Anne's eyes stayed on Tom. 'I'm sure the producer has already thought of the publicity.' Why else would he want her when he already knew what a terrible actress she was? Her abysmal performance in *Chance of a Lifetime* was the reason her mother had blackmailed his father into withdrawing the film from distribution.

Joanna's hands fluttered in the air. 'Oh, dear, I meant to help, but I seem to have made matters worse.'

'No, Mother, you've been more honest with me than Tom was.'

'Are you sure about that?'

His curt question caught her by surprise. 'What do you mean?'

Joanna looked frightened. 'Now, Tom...'

He swung on her. 'I think it's time you told Anne the rest of this.'

All the fight seemed to go out of her mother. For the first time, she looked close to her fifty years, and the sight unnerved Anne. Instead of petite and fragile, Joanna suddenly looked small and frail, and she was alarmed. 'Stop it, Tom,' she pleaded. 'Can't you see you're upsetting her?'

'You're forgetting what a great actress she is,' he said tautly. 'If there was an Oscar for avoiding the consequences of your actions, Joanna Flame would win it hands down.'

To her horror, Anne watched as tears slid out of the corners of her mother's eyes. Joanna could cry on cue, she knew, but there was something alarmingly genuine about these tears.

'It's all right, dear,' she said when Anne moved towards her. 'He's right, I have been selfish—but you must remember that I love you. You're all I have in the world.'

Enough was enough. 'You needn't go on, Mother,' Anne said. 'I know whatever you did in the past was for my benefit, so there's no point torturing yourself with it now.' Her pointed look was aimed squarely at Tom. He had a legitimate grievance against Joanna, but humiliating the woman like this wasn't going to change anything.

'It's not true, Dee—I mean, Anne,' Joanna contradicted, earning a startled look from Anne. 'I told myself it was for your own good, but it wasn't. It was for mine.'

A cold feeling of dread invaded Anne's body. 'What are you talking about?'

Joanna fumbled in her handbag and pulled out a lace handkerchief, dabbing her eyes with it. 'I have to get back to my hotel. You tell her, Tom—

I can't. If she still wants to talk to me afterwards, she can call me there.'

Before Anne could summon a protest, Joanna slammed out of the bachelor flat. Anne gripped the back of a chair and regarded Tom coldly. 'I hope you're satisfied now? It takes a great deal to reduce my mother to tears.'

'Or a weight on her conscience,' he said. He seemed unperturbed by the scene, as if he had in some way expected it.

'You mean because of what she did to your father?'

He shook his head. 'I mean because of what she did to you.'

Still cold, Anne hugged her arms around herself in an unconsciously defensive gesture. 'I admit she isn't the world's greatest mother, but she loves me. It was to provide for me after my father died that she...'

'She put up with people like me,' he said coldly when her voice trailed off. 'I hate to destroy your illusion of a heroic, self-sacrificing mother, but there's one detail she neglected to share with you.'

Speaking had become an effort, but she forced herself to ask, 'What detail?'

'You're a better actress than she'll ever be.'

It was the last thing she had expected him to say, and laughter bubbled up in her throat, refusing to be suppressed. 'Are you mad? I can't act—I never could.'

His steady gaze never left her face. 'You were told you couldn't, but it was a lie, dreamed up by your mother because she was afraid your career would eclipse hers if she encouraged it.'

'I don't believe you.'

'I didn't expect you to, but I can prove it. Get your things. You're coming back to the hotel with me.'

How could she go anywhere with him ever again, knowing how he had used her? He had allowed her to think he cared when all he wanted was to persuade her to take a part in his film. It might not be the casting couch she remembered, but as a modern version it took some beating. She shook her head in fierce denial. 'I'm not going anywhere with you, now or any other time.'

With exaggerated patience, he folded his arms across his broad chest. 'There are two ways we can do this, the easy way or the hard way. Which do you prefer?'

Shaken by his determination, Anne wavered. 'You can't make me come with you.'

His gimlet eyes bored into her. 'What exactly is it that you're afraid of?'

Her hair tossed in a futile gesture of defiance. 'I'm not afraid of anything.'

'Then you shouldn't object to discovering the truth about yourself.'

She already knew the truth. She had seen the rushes of *Chances of a Lifetime* for herself, and they proved that she was a terrible actress. Surely Tom wouldn't humiliate her by making her sit through that awful film? When it was finished her mother had offered to bring home a print, but Anne had refused. She had seen enough in the editing-room to last her a lifetime.

'It won't change anything,' she insisted, 'but if it's the only way to end this I'll come. Then I'm going back to work for Sam. I never want to see you again or have anything more to do with your film.'

If he saw through her brave lie, he said nothing as they drove back to his hotel. The thought of never seeing him again filled her with despair. Foolishly, she had fallen in love with him, and nothing could erase the emotional pain that racked her at finding out how he had used her.

It was her own stupid fault, she acknowledged, although it didn't ease the ache inside her. She had known who and what he was from the moment they met, but had been swept along on a current of desire so strong that she had been powerless to resist.

She had seen what she wanted to see in him, read what she wanted to read in his kisses. None of it was real. He had callously manipulated her to get what he wanted. And he had succeeded beyond his wildest dreams.

Her eyes brimmed and she closed them tightly, not wanting to give him the satisfaction of her tears. Thank goodness she hadn't told him how she felt. He need never know about the flames that leapt inside her at his touch, or the liquid fire that tore along her veins when she was in his arms. Her heart felt leaden as she tormented herself with memories that she recognised now as artfully orchestrated lies.

'You've got it all wrong,' Tom insisted, as if he could read her mind.

'Does it matter?'

'It does to me.'

She twisted as far around as her seatbelt allowed. 'Are you going to deny that you wanted me for your film from the first?'

His fingers drummed an impatient tattoo on the steering-wheel, the same long fingers she had fantasised about last night. 'I don't deny it. You're perfect for the part.'

'So you set about convincing me, didn't you?'

'Not in the way you mean.'

Her sigh whispered between them. 'What's the point of arguing? We both know it happens all the time. I just want to get this over with.'

'Suit yourself,' he said through tightly clenched teeth.

If she could suit herself she would be miles away from here, assaying mineral samples in some remote mining area. Tom's high-handed behaviour, making her relive a hated part of her past, made her ache with unshed tears. He was a user of people, a manipulator, just like all the rest. The only difference was, she loved him, so the hurt was beyond measuring.

She was hardly aware of taking the lift to the penthouse suite. She just wanted this to be over so that she could pick up the pieces of her life and start yet again. No matter what the film revealed— and doubts were starting to creep in—she wanted no part of his film.

In a haze of misery, she saw him make a telephone call, then he hung up and turned to her. 'I've ordered breakfast to be sent up to the suite.'

'I'm not hungry,' she said automatically. Her stomach rebelled at the very idea of food.

'All the same, you'll think more clearly after you've eaten something.'

She was already thinking more clearly than she wanted to, and she felt sick at the thought of how she had nearly given herself to him last night. If it hadn't been for the children sleeping in the next room, she would have done. How could she have lived with herself then?

A video player was set up on top of a television set, and she watched impassively as Tom dropped a cassette into the machine and picked up a remote control. 'You can sit down, you know. This won't be the ordeal you expect.'

'It's hardly a picnic, either.' Nevertheless, she sat down at the far end of the couch, her whole body hunched into a posture of defeat. The fact that he had a video cassette of her film in his possession reminded her vividly that he had planned this from the start.

Knowing it didn't stop her pulses from racing as he slid his arm along the back of the couch, stopping just short of her shoulder. She retreated into her corner, wishing she could control her responses as easily as he controlled the tape player.

She kept her eyes averted from the screen. What on earth was she doing here? She knew what the film would show. Nothing had changed since it was made.

Tom leaned forward. 'This is the part I particularly want you to see,' he told her.

As if he controlled it, her gaze was dragged to the television set and remained there, her eyes widening with astonishment, as she saw what he meant. She had been playing a young actress, cast in a part which hundreds of seasoned performers were vying for. Her character had been accused of sleeping her way into the role, but was actually the producer's estranged daughter, a fact neither of them discovered until well into the picture.

Something *had* changed since the film was made. 'This isn't the footage I watched in the editing-room,' she said, puzzled.

'I didn't think so. What you saw were out-takes, not suitable for use in the finished film.'

Puzzled, Anne shifted her focus to Tom. 'Why was I told it was usable film?'

He made an explosive noise of frustration. 'Under pressure, every actor blows a line now and then or gets a movement wrong. Those bits are filmed along with the scenes in which everything goes perfectly. If you only saw the mistakes, what would you think?'

'That I was clumsy and useless, that I couldn't act.' Her voice was thick with emotion. Why would anyone do such a thing to her?

'And what do you think now?'

She concentrated on the girl on the screen—herself eight years ago. No amount of trying to be objective could obscure the truth. The girl *was* the young actress, discovering her long-lost father. The emotion she generated on the screen was so real that it was almost palpable. Playing the part, Anne had drawn on her own feelings of loss at her father's death, and what she saw now was so convincing that a lump rose in her throat.

She turned brimming eyes to Tom. 'I don't know what to say.'

'Yes, you do, because the truth is there in front of you. That girl is a born actress.'

She felt as if someone had revealed a part of herself to be a monster. 'It was one part, a fluke. It doesn't mean anything.'

'It means you have a rare talent, given to only a handful of people in a generation. Your mother recognised it, and it frightened her so much she couldn't handle it.'

'Maybe she was right. It hasn't brought her happiness.'

Dropping the remote control, Tom slid across to her and grasped her hands tightly. 'Is that what you're afraid of, the unhappiness you think will come from using your God-given talents?'

It had already brought her unhappiness, she thought wildly, straining to escape from his grasp. If it were not for this so-called talent, Tom wouldn't have come looking for her and she wouldn't have to deal with the consequences of falling in love with him. 'Can't you leave me alone?' she asked, feeling wetness staining her flushed cheeks.

'No, I can't. What you have is too rare and precious to hide. You owe it to the world.'

She wrenched her hands free. Her eyes were suddenly bleak. 'What you mean is, I owe it to you.'

His brows hunched together. 'What's that supposed to mean?'

With icy clarity, Anne finally understood what was going on. 'I think you know. Because of what happened to your father, you think I owe you something, and this is your way of collecting.'

'I can understand you thinking so,' Tom said in a flat voice. 'I did have it in mind when I thought you were responsible for my father's death. When

I found out that your mother was acting alone, I changed my thinking.'

'Before or after you decided to seduce me?'

'Now just a minute, one has nothing to do with the other.'

'Forgive me if I find it hard to believe.'

He stood up, his eyes blazing. 'I won't forgive you, because you're totally wrong. Perhaps your mother's lessons have rubbed off and you think this is how we do business in the film industry, but I don't.'

She couldn't, wouldn't let herself believe that his kisses were genuine. All that mattered was her agreement to play the part in his film. The remembered closeness was a convenient fiction, and she felt raw knowing that she was the only one who believed it.

'It doesn't matter anyway,' she said, the blatant lie sounding convincing, which was a wonder, given her see-sawing emotions. 'You've won.'

Never had his blue eyes looked so arctic. 'How so?' he asked.

'I'll make the film.' When he started to interrupt, she held up a hand. 'Let me finish. It will be my first and last film, under my real name of Anne Fleming. There's to be no publicity about Joanna Flame's daughter. I stand or fall on my own merits.'

She had expected triumph, but his expression was stony. 'To what do I owe this change of heart?'

'To the fact that there's a debt to be paid here. Whatever her motives, my mother's actions were wrong, and your father paid a terrible price. I can't undo the damage, but this is something I can do to help make amends.'

She glimpsed admiration in the flinty gaze, before his eyelids hooded them. 'Even though the debt isn't yours to pay?'

'It was done in my name.'

'Very well, then. I agree to your conditions.'

Never had she felt so coldly in control of herself. Later, she knew the dam would burst and the hurt would come flooding through, but for now she needed calm. 'There's one more condition,' she told him.

A flicker of interest lit his blue gaze. 'I'm listening.'

'During filming, if you so much as touch me, other than in the course of my work, I walk off the picture and don't come back.'

'What in hell kind of condition is that, after what we've shared together?'

She ignored the implication that he had shared her feelings. She wanted to believe it, but knew in her heart how impossible it was. Now that he had achieved his goal, she was surprised he wanted to keep up the fiction. 'All the same, it's my condition,' she re-stated.

Tom's mouth tightened into a grim line. 'You drive a hard bargain, Anne, but I agree.'

He couldn't know it, but it was hardest of all on herself, she thought. How could she work with him, talk to him, be near him day after day and pretend to be indifferent to him? It would be the biggest acting challenge of her life.

Groping for her handbag, she stood up. 'I'll have to go,' she said. 'Sam needs to know my plans so he can replace me while I work on the film.'

'Breakfast should be here any minute.'

She had no appetite. More than anything, she wanted to get out of here while she retained some vestige of self-control. She had said she was going to see Sam, but first she meant to go home and cry her eyes out. She felt as if she was holding herself together by a thread. He reached for her, and she gave a cry of anguish. 'Don't touch me.'

He was the stronger and pulled her shaking body against him. 'I can't let you leave like this.'

She lifted her tear-streaked face to him. 'Why not? You got what you wanted.'

'What you *think* I want,' he ground out. '*This* is what I really want.'

His smouldering look should have warned her of his intent, but nothing prepared her for the onslaught of his mouth against hers. More an act of possession than a kiss, it buried her protests under an avalanche of erotic sensations she was powerless to withstand.

Shivers of desire rippled through her and she clung weakly to him while he ravaged her mouth with a thoroughness she had never experienced before. His hands dug into her back, and she felt his ardour as a hot, pulsating force against her stomach. Explosions of desire rocketed through her. In spite of everything, she still wanted him.

The couch pressed against the back of her knees, buckling them. She was already angled backwards by the force of his embrace. It would be so easy to sink down and he would follow, covering her body with his. Everything in her ached to enfold him, to be possessed by him in the most elemental way.

His voice reached her from a long way away. 'God, Anne, this is how I dreamed it would be.'

Dreamed or planned? Was she too part of the price he had intended to extract for the death of his father? He had already achieved one aim. Was she stupidly making it easy for him to achieve the other?

The fear that she could be right turned her to stone in his arms. He felt the change and frowned down at her. 'Did I say something wrong?'

'No, you said something right. You reminded me of why I'm here.'

'You're here because I want you here,' he murmured, moving his lips seductively across her temple. She shivered as tendrils of desire wound around her consciousness. He wanted her, not out of love, but to extract his revenge, she reminded herself. Well, she still had her pride. He wasn't having it all his own way.

She slid out of the circle of his arms. 'You're forgetting my last condition.'

His arms dropped to his sides, but his hands were clenched into fists as he strove to keep his voice level. 'You forgot it too, while you were in my arms.'

She could forget her own name under those conditions, she thought as the room spun crazily for a moment. She grabbed the back of a chair to steady herself. This would have to stop. 'Nevertheless, I'm not part of our bargain,' she insisted. 'Otherwise I can't do the film.'

Tom's expression turned thunderous and he slammed a fist into the palm of his other hand.

'Damn you, Anne. You know this film needs you. I have to agree to your conditions, even though I don't think it's what either of us really wants.'

Her heart pounded against the wall of her chest. He made it sound as if he shared her feelings. Was it more of his clever manipulation? She dared not take the risk. Her voice held a pleading note as she said, 'You'll stand by our agreement?'

'I will, because you leave me no choice.' Tom's breath whistled out in a heavy sigh. 'Very well, Anne, I won't touch you again unless it's in the line of duty.'

It was what she wanted, but she felt as if she'd lost something precious in gaining his promise. She tried to tell herself it would simplify matters. If he didn't touch her, there could be no repeat of the last mind-shattering few minutes, no chance that she would forget who and what he was and let him make love to her.

The tension-laden moment was broken by a rap on the door and a muffled announcement, 'Room service.'

She almost collided with the breakfast cart as she raced for the door and flung it open, squeezing past the startled waiter before Tom could stop her.

CHAPTER EIGHT

'So THIS is where you're hiding. I came to let you know we're starting rehearsals this afternoon. Everything OK?'

Anne started as Tom appeared in the doorway. He had kept his promise not to touch her, but she hadn't expected to feel so bereft. No matter how she told herself she was doing the right thing, she still hungered for the warmth of his arms and the heady power of his kisses. Working together promised to be sheer torment, but she was committed now. She would have to hide her feelings as best she could if she was to salvage anything of her pride.

'I'm quite comfortable, thanks,' she assured him, trying to keep the strain out of her voice. Talking about inconsequential things seemed to help, so she plunged on. 'Emerald Station's a lovely place. Someone told me it was built in 1878.'

He nodded. 'It would have been a one-roomed cottage then, of course. But they've kept the extensions in the colonial style to preserve the atmosphere. It's the main reason I wanted some of the cast to come here to start blocking out *Kalgoorlie Gold*.'

She could see his point. He had wanted the cast to experience the goldfields atmosphere, and where better than in authentic Victorian surroundings? Anne's room was delightful, with its magnificent

brass bedstead, timber washstand and repro-
duction Victorian decorations. Under other, less
emotion-charged circumstances, she would have
enjoyed staying at the homestead very much.

'I saw your mother the other day,' he said,
breaking into her thoughts.

She gave him a startled look. 'You did? Why?'

'I wanted her to know that I forgive her for what
she did to my father. I've accepted that she didn't
know about his weak heart.'

A lump rose in her throat. 'Your forgiveness will
mean a lot to her. It was very generous of you.'

Tom gestured dismissively. 'It wasn't generous.
It was the right thing to do, and I did it.'

'All the same, I'm sure you eased her mind a lot.'
She didn't add that she had been terribly worried
about Joanna since she'd arrived in Kalgoorlie. Her
mother looked far from well. But despite his
gesture, Anne didn't think Tom would be interested
in her family concerns. He had done the right thing
as he saw it, and now it was over.

His gaze went to the typewritten pages lying on
her bed. 'Now you've had time to study it, what
do you think of the script?' he asked.

'It's brilliant,' she said unhesitatingly.

He inclined his head. 'Thank you. I'm glad you
like my work.'

A wave of weakness washed over Anne. '*You*
wrote the script?'

'I gather you don't know that Thomas Howson
is my pen-name,' he said drily.

'No, I didn't.' Howard's son. Yes, she could see
the connection now. She'd read several marvellous

Australian historical thrillers by the same author, never suspecting that he was really Tom Callander.

Hot colour flooded her cheeks. The author was famous for his graphic sex scenes. While they were never gratuitous, they were uncomfortably detailed, and she felt embarrassed at the thought of Tom knowing she'd read them.

Were they written from first-hand experience? The thought came unbidden into her mind. Maybe the gossip columns were right after all. Then an even more appalling thought struck her. Were all his kisses part of his ongoing research? The thought that her responses might one day appear in one of his books mortified her. Thank goodness they'd gone no further—at least there was a limit to what he could write about her.

Her thoughts must have shown on her face, because he gave a throaty chuckle. 'Now you're wondering whether or not I kiss and tell,' he said softly.

'And do you?'

'You'll have to read Thomas Howson's next thriller to find out.'

Tears of frustration sparkled in her eyes and she swung away towards the window. Desperate to change the subject which had become much too personal for comfort, she asked over her shoulder, 'Did my mother know you were coming to Kalgoorlie to see me?'

'Of course. She told me where to find you.'

She spun around, anger replacing the tears in her eyes. 'She what? How could she do that to me?'

Tom shrugged. 'I'd have tracked you down anyway after finding your picture in the local paper. I only went to Joanna to find out why you gave up acting, and for some reason, she decided to tell me the truth.'

The colour drained from Anne's face. 'She was using me to appease her conscience. It's what she meant when she said it isn't too late to make amends. She meant through me, didn't she?'

'Maybe not. Maybe she wanted to make up for the harm she'd caused the two of us over the years.'

She wanted to believe it, but doubt warred inside her. Her mother couldn't know how much more harm her intended remedy had caused. Joanna didn't suspect that Anne had stupidly fallen in love with Tom when he was only interested in her as Katie Dooley, the young lover in his film.

Tom seemed about to say more, but they were interrupted by one of the Emerald Station staff, calling Anne to the public telephone in the hall. She was aware of Tom's soft-footed departure as she picked up the receiver. It was Joanna.

'I called to see how you're getting on,' she said when Anne greeted her.

'I'm fine, Mother,' Anne said automatically. She was no saint. Forgiving her mother for what she had done would take time, and there was an air of tension between them which hadn't existed before, despite Anne's attempt to act normally.

'I'm glad. Tom explained why he wanted you all there together. Who else is staying with you?'

Anne mentioned a few actors whose names her mother would know, and Joanna murmured an acknowledgement, adding, 'I'm so glad you decided to take the part.'

Tension stiffened Anne's spine. 'I'm sure you are.'

'Please don't hold it against me, darling,' her mother pleaded down the phone. 'Now you know how good you are, you must understand why I panicked?'

Anne sighed. 'There's no point going over it, is there? What's done is done.'

'All the same, you have a right to hate me.'

'I've already told you I don't hate you, Mother. It's just that sometimes you make it hard for me to like you. I'll have to go soon.'

Her mother's voice brightened. 'Tom's waiting, I take it? He's a remarkable young man, isn't he? Or isn't thirty-one considered young any more? At any rate, you could do worse.'

Colour leached into Anne's cheeks, but she kept her voice steady. 'Stop it, Mother! I'm not interested in Tom, not romantically, anyway.' She hoped her voice didn't betray the blatant lie.

Her mother murmured sympathetically, 'Pity. Still, it's probably just as well, if Sylvie Sheridan's there.'

Sylvie Sheridan played Marcia, Katie Dooley's friend and confidante in the film. 'Why is it just as well because Sylvie's here?' she couldn't resist asking.

'Of course, you're out of touch with the industry gossip. Sylvie and Tom have been an item for ages. I'm sure they'd have married if Sylvie's first husband had agreed to a divorce. He wants to re-marry now, so the way's clear for her and Tom.'

Anne was glad her mother couldn't see her shocked expression. Sylvie and Tom. It was so ob-vious that she was amazed she hadn't noticed it before. The closeness between them had been obvious from the moment Sylvie arrived. Tom had draped an arm around her shoulders as he made the introductions. And Sylvie herself had made it clear to Anne that she thought they had been given the wrong roles.

'I'm sure the role of Katie will be mine as soon as Tom realises his mistake,' she had said. Anne had put it down to professional jealousy, but there was more, much more. Sylvie thought she should be working closely with Tom on the more complex role.

The irony of it was, Sylvie was worried for nothing. Tom had already promised Anne he wouldn't touch her unless it was in the line of duty. Now she knew why he had agreed to her condition so readily. He had known all along that Sylvie's divorce was almost through, so he wasn't going to be lonely for long.

Her mother's news confirmed Anne's suspicion that Tom's kisses had been his way of ensuring she took the part. Now she had agreed, he and Sylvie could continue where they left off.

It was all perfectly logical and understandable, so why did Anne feel so shattered suddenly? It wasn't as if she didn't know his type. There was no reason for the sick feeling which assailed her.

She told herself it was nausea at discovering the truth about him. Hadn't his name been linked with Sylvie's *before* her divorce came through? He was every bit as unprincipled as Anne suspected, yet it didn't assuage the longing she felt whenever she thought about him.

'Are you still there, darling?' Joanna's anxious voice brought her back to the present.

'I'm here,' she said with an effort. 'I'm a bit tired, that's all. It must be the upheaval of moving here and getting started on the film.'

She hadn't wanted to live at Emerald Station at all, insisting that she could commute from Kalgoorlie each day. But Tom had insisted, saying it would waste time and undermine the team spirit he wanted to build.

It also meant spending every day and evening in his company, but Anne didn't want to admit that it was the main reason why she had resisted the idea.

'Maybe a change of scene will be good for you,' her mother suggested.

Anne sighed. 'You could be right. But I feel guilty being here instead of looking after you.'

'I don't need looking after,' Joanna said with a sharpness that startled Anne.

'I'm sorry. I only meant . . .'

'I know, and I didn't mean to snap,' Joanna cut in. 'But I came to see you and enjoy myself, not get under your feet.'

'You aren't underfoot,' Anne insisted. 'There's so much to see in the goldfields, and I'd love to show it to you.'

'I know, darling, but this is important too. I hear that the première's going to benefit your youth centre.'

Anne brightened considerably. 'It's another reason why I'm doing the film, to help the kids. They really need a place of their own. In the mining industry, their parents move around so much that they don't get a chance to socialise properly.'

'Like you and me,' Joanna mused. 'I took you with me as much as I could, thinking only of the benefits to you, not of the disruption to your life.'

'We survived, didn't we?'

Joanna chuckled. 'We sure did, kiddo. Well, I have to go now. Your boss is showing me around the Golden Mile.'

'I'm glad,' said Anne, relief in her tone. 'You'll have a good time.'

Sam had been wonderful about giving her leave to make the film. He had offered to keep her on the company payroll, although she had assured him she would be well paid for her role. The saving on her salary might help the company too. She also reluctantly agreed with Sam that the publicity surrounding the film wouldn't hurt either.

Already there was a degree of interest in her 'sudden' rise to stardom. Only Sam knew about her relationship to Joanna, and he promised to keep it to himself. Joanna had already been recognised, of course, but so far no one had connected her and Anne. It would come, but she decided to deal with it when it happened.

'"Sufficient unto the day is the evil thereof,"' she recalled her father saying when she was small. He had been right. Coping with the film was enough without looking too far ahead, something she hardly dared to do since it inevitably involved facing a future without Tom.

'Have a good time sightseeing,' she told her mother.

'I will, darling. I love you.'

'I love you too.' Anne felt a strange unease as she hung up the phone. What was the matter with her mother? She had sounded unusually fragile and unsure of herself, not like the Joanna Flame Anne was used to. She must have been working too hard, Anne concluded, glad after all that Joanna had come to the outback for a break. It was obviously much needed.

Returning to her room, Anne leaned out of the window, breathing in the fragrant country air. The day was much too glorious to spend inside, and she had already studied her script until the print blurred before her eyes. The property possessed a tennis court shaded by leafy gum trees, but it was deserted. Then voices floated up to her from the old shearing shed which housed a swimming-pool, sauna and showers. Her decision was made.

Moments later she had changed into a navy blue one-piece bathing suit, slipped a terry-towelling dress over the top and picked up a towel. A swim seemed like a wonderful idea.

But when she let herself into the shearing shed and saw who was using the pool she immediately regretted her impulse. There was a ball game in progress, and Sylvie Sheridan's blonde hair bobbed in the water as she caught the ball Tom tossed to her.

'Enough!' she shrieked, wrapping her arms around the ball to keep herself afloat. 'You win, all right?'

'As long as you agree it's on points, not sufferance,' laughed Tom. He caught sight of Anne hovering uncertainly at the entrance of the shed. 'Coming in, Anne?'

'I'm not sure. I only came to take a look.'

His gaze flicked to the towel she clutched in both hands. 'You look as if you mean business. We've been getting some exercise, but my team-mate has collapsed, so the pool's all yours.'

Sylvie aimed the ball at him. 'I'll show you who's collapsed.'

She swam away, and Tom followed, ploughing through the water like an Olympic champion. When he caught up with Sylvie, he pretended to duck her, until she clasped her arms around his neck in surrender. He didn't seem to mind.

She would have to get used to the sight, Anne thought, although misery welled up inside her at the idea. Would it always be this hard?

With grim determination, she shed her cover-up and dropped it with her towel on to one of the loungers beside the pool. Then she dived into the deep end, well away from Tom and Sylvie, and swam lap after dogged lap until she could hardly lift her arms.

The exercise dissipated some of her tension, but she was shivering with exhaustion by the time she dragged herself out of the water. Tom was in the sauna, she saw, spotting him through the glass picture window.

Her breath caught in her throat at the sight of his muscular shape, the lower half wrapped in a towel. Moisture beaded his upper body and his hair was slicked to his head. He looked like a statue of a Greek god.

Returning to her towel, Anne rubbed herself down, then dropped on to the lounger, closing her eyes against a wave of pain that threatened to engulf her. The barrier between them was as solid as the

glass window. She had made Tom promise not to
touch her, when she was the one who longed to
touch him. Knowing how he had used her should
have strengthened her resistance, but even reminding herself of it didn't seem to help.

'Quite the athletic type, aren't you?' said a voice
close beside her. 'I'd be afraid of developing too
many muscles. They're hardly feminine, are they?'

Looking at Sylvie's reed-slim body encased in the
briefest black bikini Anne had ever seen, she
doubted whether muscles would ever be Sylvie's
problem. Nor would a lack of femininity. She fairly
oozed it, from the top of her fluffy blonde mane
to the tips of her perfectly manicured toes. 'I don't
think you need to worry,' she said.

'Thanks,' murmured Sylvie as if it was a compliment. Maybe it was. 'This is a heavenly pool,
isn't it? I didn't expect such luxury in the middle
of nowhere.'

'Kalgoorlie's hardly the middle of nowhere,
except perhaps geographically,' Anne countered,
defending her adopted home town. 'It's a fully
fledged city with all the usual amenities. And it has
a wonderful community spirit.'

Sylvie eased her shoulder straps down, revealing
evenly tanned shoulders with no signs of strap
marks. She must sunbathe topless, Anne thought,
fighting a touch of envy. What was the matter with
her? She had never envied any woman's looks
before, being content with her sharp brain and an
appearance which she considered adequate,
although her mother said she undervalued herself.

'I've heard about your community spirit,' Sylvie said, interrupting her thoughts. 'Aren't you involved in some kind of youth project yourself?'

Masking her surprise at Sylvie's interest, Anne said, 'I'm helping to raise funds for a drop-in centre. Tom's film première is going to help a lot.'

She wasn't sure why she added this last, unless it was to remind Sylvie that Tom wasn't exclusively hers.

Sylvie chewed her full lower lip. 'Tom's a generous man. Some people mistake his generosity for something more personal.'

Was she being warned off? Debating whether to assure Sylvie that a warning was unnecessary, Anne decided to ignore it. Sylvie would soon find out that Anne was no threat to her.

'Keeping kids out of trouble seems to be a big job these days. At their age, I was already married.'

The sudden admission made Anne look at Sylvie in surprise. 'You must have married young. What went wrong?' she asked.

'Boredom, mainly. Jeff was a successful businessman and there was no room in his life for my career. I couldn't handle the little-wifey routine, so when it came to a choice between him and my work the work won.'

'I'm sorry,' Anne murmured.

Sylvie waved an airy hand. 'No need—it was valuable experience. He's finally giving me a divorce after all this time.'

Anne went cold as she realised where the conversation had been leading from the first. 'So I hear,' she said in a strained voice.

Her companion grinned. 'The grapevine reaches all the way out here, does it?' She leaned closer. 'Then you also know it's what we've been waiting for.'

Anne's throat tightened and a band of pain wound itself around her chest. 'I know,' she admitted.

'Good. Then we understand each other, don't we?'

In a graceful move, Sylvie stood up, wound a towel around her body and walked towards the sauna.

The group was assembling for lunch on the enclosed veranda which enabled guests to enjoy the view without being bothered by flies. After the meal, they were to start rehearsals in earnest.

After the scene at the pool, Anne would have preferred to eat alone in her room, but she didn't want to be thought stand-offish, so she made herself join the others as soon as she had changed out of her swimming things.

Miles Davidson, the actor who played Herbert Hoover, was already in conversation with Andrew Aragon, the black actor who played Coyle, the Aboriginal leader. Anne returned their greetings, but sat down at an empty table, pretending interest in some lambs which were being hand-fed in a paddock near the homestead.

She was picking desultorily at her lunch of spinach quiche and deep-fried mushrooms when Tom slid into the seat opposite her. 'I'll have the same,' he told the waitress who materialised at his elbow. 'It looks good.'

Trying to control the tension that vibrated through her at his presence, Anne gave a casual nod. 'I'm told everything is grown here, even the wild salad—which is delicious, by the way.'

She was rambling, she knew, but seemed unable to stop herself. With his hair slick from the pool and his skin glowing from the sauna, Tom looked incredibly attractive. Food, however delicious, came a poor second.

When his food was placed in front of him, he ate appreciatively, so there was no need to strive for conversation. Expecting Sylvie to join them at any moment, Anne ate quickly, intending to slip away. She had no wish to hear any more of Sylvie's warnings about Tom, nor to witness their closeness, which she acknowledged was the real problem.

Tom lifted a napkin to his mouth, then lowered the fabric square, his eyes appraising as he regarded her over the top. 'I gather that you and Sylvie aren't getting along too well,' he remarked.

'Who told you that? Sylvie?' No doubt she couldn't wait to complain to Tom about some fancied slight, although Anne had kept out of the other woman's way so far.

'She didn't have to.' He glanced around to ensure they couldn't be overheard. 'The tension between you speaks for itself. But I won't allow it to disrupt this project.'

Or upset his current favourite, she put her own interpretation on the warning. She had a mental picture of them together in the sauna, and her stomach lurched. It was quite clear whose side Tom would take in an argument. 'I understand,' she said miserably. 'Although I didn't really need the warning. I'm well aware of how things stand.'

'You also thought you couldn't act,' he told her mildly. He reached for the menu. 'I think I'll have the brandied fruit and home-made ice-cream for dessert. What about you?'

Anne dropped her crumpled napkin on to the table. 'I've had all I can handle,' she said, wondering if he was aware of the double meaning. She was aware of his frown boring into her as she left the table.

Rehearsals were being held in the old woolshed next door to the converted shearing quarters. Although the woolshed was now officially a conference centre, it retained much of its character, with high vaulted ceilings and timber-lined walls. An unobtrusive air-conditioning system made the temperature comfortable.

Carrying her script, Anne took a seat in the back row of a circle of chairs and studied her lines while she waited for the others. Andrew Aragon was the first to arrive, followed by Miles Davidson, then Sylvie and Tom, deep in conversation.

Noting the closeness of the two heads, Anne bit her lip. How was she ever going to get through this ordeal, far less give a creditable performance, when every sense ran riot as soon as Tom came into the room?

He quickly brought the group to order. 'We'll start with the scene between Katie and Marcus, when they first discover they love each other,' he announced.

'But Marcus—I mean, Trevor—can't get here until tomorrow,' Sylvie put in.

He gave her an irritated frown. 'I'm aware of Trevor's absence. This is just to get the feel of the script. I'll read Marcus's part myself for now.'

Oh, no, he couldn't expect her to act out a love scene with him, could he? Anne thought in dismay. 'Perhaps we should start with some of the others,' she said diffidently.

'Someone has to be first, and you're the most out of practice, which is why I suggested starting with you,' he said. 'The others will get their turn.'

His argument made sense, but it didn't stop the flurry of nerves that gripped her. She had forgotten the torment of these early rehearsals when everyone was feeling their way. How could she have let herself be talked into this?

She was repaying her mother's debt to Tom, she reminded herself. After what Joanna had done to his father in her name, she owed him her best performance. She squared her shoulders as she found the page he wanted and moved to the front of the room.

Still, the words of love she was expected to say to Marcus stalled in her throat when she tried to address them to Tom. They were so much what she wanted to say to him that her vocal cords closed on the words.

He moved closer and slid an arm around her shoulders. 'Relax, it's only a read-through.'

Panic flared in her eyes and her whole body tensed. 'You promised you wouldn't touch me.'

'Unless it's in the line of duty,' he reminded her. 'And this qualifies.'

She wasn't Anne, she was Katie Dooley, she told herself frantically. It wasn't Tom holding her but

Marcus, her own dear love. At the thought, she felt her body soften and become more pliant, moulding itself to Tom's hard contours.

He felt the change at once. 'That's the idea. Now tell me how much you care,' he prompted.

'I love you more than life itself,' she quoted, putting all the love she felt for Tom into the line. Never mind that he believed she was acting. She knew she meant the words with all her heart, and they rang sweetly with conviction as a result.

The rest of the speech came out fluently, charged with all the emotion she felt for Tom. By the time she finished, he was regarding her oddly, his expression unfathomable.

A burst of spontaneous applause shattered the moment, and she looked at the others in confusion. Then Tom joined in. 'It's well deserved,' he said warmly. 'You gave a stunning performance, and I take back what I said about your being out of practice.'

She was aware of Sylvie's furious glare following her back to her seat. 'You played Katie like a lovesick puppy,' she muttered under her breath, but Anne caught the words. Did Sylvie guess what motivation Anne had used? She hoped not, because the scene had nothing to do with reality, or so she kept reminding herself.

Miserably, she tried to concentrate as Andrew Aragon and Tom read a scene together. The young assistant had been hiding the Aboriginal fugitive at great risk to himself, and Coyle had made Marcus a totem to show his gratitude.

Watching the scene, Anne felt a sense of detachment. She was glad that the actor playing

Marcus would arrive soon, so she wouldn't have to do any more scenes with Tom. He was a superb actor, but there was too much between them for her to concentrate on her role while he shared the same stage.

It was almost more than she could bear to see Sylvie join Tom for a read-through of her scene. Strictly speaking, Tom wasn't involved in this scene, but Sylvie prettily insisted that it would work better if he took the other part. 'Only until I get my bearings,' she said.

'Sylvie, my love, you know I can't refuse you anything,' Tom said with an apologetic shrug at the actor who should have read the part. 'But it's just for today, right?'

The actress fluttered her eyelashes at him, making Anne feel faintly ill. 'Thanks, darling. I knew you'd understand. Are we still on for tonight?'

There were several ribald comments among the cast, and Anne held her breath as Tom said, 'Settle down, everyone. And yes, Sylvie, I will help you with your script this evening.'

Despite the air-conditioning, the room became stifling suddenly. Not waiting to hear any more, Anne picked up her script, murmured an excuse and hurried outside.

CHAPTER NINE

'WHERE are we up to?' Anne whispered to Miles Davidson as she took a seat beside him.

From the front, Tom's look of annoyance raked her, and she shrank into the seat. She was just as cross with herself for being late for rehearsal as he obviously was, but it was his fault anyway.

Picturing him working late into the night with Sylvie had kept her awake for hours. As a result, she had slept through breakfast and reached the woolshed after rehearsals began.

'It's only ten minutes,' she muttered under her breath.

Miles heard her and smiled. 'Tom's a perfectionist, like his father. But it shows in the finished product, so we should be grateful.'

'You're right,' she said on a sigh. 'But it doesn't make him easy to work with.' It was even harder if you were in love with him, she added inwardly.

'Genius is seldom easy to get along with,' Miles said in a sanguine tone.

Tom was busy conferring with the others, so she decided to ask Miles a question which had been nagging at her. 'Just what is Tom's role in this production? He seems to be producer, director and actor all in one.'

Miles gave a low chuckle. 'He'll probably direct in the end, once he's finished experimenting with the script. I can't see him trusting a Howson script to another director.'

Her eyebrows lifted. 'You know about Thomas Howson?'

'It's an open secret in the industry.'

Like Tom's relationship with Sylvie Sheridan, Anne thought, shifting on her hard chair. Why couldn't they make these things padded, so skinny people didn't have to suffer? she thought in passing.

Then she faced the fact that the real source of her discomfort was Sylvie and Tom. Linking their names together in her mind sent a shaft of pain through her chest, making her want to clutch a hand to it.

'Writer, director, actor—I wish I had half his talent,' Miles mused, watching as Tom skilfully guided Andrew and Sylvie through a difficult scene.

Anne's gaze shifted back to Miles. 'You needn't worry, you're very good. I enjoyed the TV series where you played the judge in the country court.'

'It was a good role, but film is my first love.' He leaned closer, keeping his words between them. 'You're good too. Where have you been hiding all your talent? This can't be your first film.'

'I grew up around the film industry,' she confessed. 'But I never wanted to be an actress. Tom persuaded me to take this role.'

'He's adept at persuasion,' Miles agreed. 'But he must think you're worth it. You do look familiar. What have I seen you in?'

There was no way to avoid the admission. 'You haven't, but you could have seen my mother, Joanna Flame.'

He looked satisfied. 'You look a little like her—which is a compliment, by the way. I gather you don't want word getting around?'

Her grateful smile answered his question. 'It's bound to get out sooner or later, but I want to do this on my own merit first.'

He nodded gravely. 'Very wise. I have a famous brother-in-law, and people assume I get parts because of the connection, so I don't publicise it.'

'I understand—I won't either,' Anne promised.

His eyes twinkled. 'Deal. You know, I thought I saw Joanna recently. I wasn't mistaken, was I?'

'No, she came to town to see me and have a break.'

'Good idea. She isn't looking well lately. The gossip around the trade says she's been ill.'

'She hasn't said anything to me.' Alarm flared through her. Could it be true? She recalled her mother's extreme thinness and the dark shadows that rimmed her eyes. She'd reacted angrily when Anne suggested taking care of her. She made up her mind to confront Joanna with her concern as soon as she could.

Miles nudged her as Sylvie flounced by, taking a seat not far from Anne. 'There's your real problem. She doesn't need an excuse to hang her jealousy on.'

'I think I got the part she wanted,' Anne murmured.

'You got the part you should have. You're perfect for Katie. With Tom as Marcus, you're dynamite together.'

A hollow feeling gripped Anne. 'He's only filling in until the real actor gets here, isn't he?'

'So he says, but the word is he wrote Marcus with himself in mind, so he isn't too worried about whether Trevor turns up or not.'

The actor hadn't arrived yet, so Tom was still reading the part of Marcus. If Miles was right, it explained why he didn't seem to mind.

Anne wished she felt the same, but saying words of love to Tom was the most exquisite torment she had ever known. Part of her rejoiced in the freedom to say what was in her heart, but another part damned her for her hypocrisy. The others credited her with acting talent, but it took no skill to say what she really meant. The only one who didn't realise it was Tom himself. And he was too pre-occupied with Sylvie to notice that Anne wasn't acting.

He came towards her, and she braced herself, but he passed by with a curt nod and a murmured, 'Glad you decided to join us.' The reference to her lateness stung and she felt her colour heighten. Her palm itched to connect with his handsome face, and she flexed her fingers before clenching them into fists.

Tom didn't notice as he swept by, saying to the group at large that he would be back after he had taken a telephone call.

As soon as he was gone, Anne relaxed. It was as if he were a live power source that sent a current pulsing through her. When he left the current was switched off and she breathed again. And this was only the beginning. How was she to survive the weeks of involvement with him that stretched ahead?

Miles touched her arm. 'Andrew wants you up there. Page seventy-six.'

She fumbled through her script and found the page, then joined Andrew at the front. In the scene, the Aboriginal, Coyle, and Katie Dooley were at his hideout not far from Niagara Dam. It was a rare moment of communion between the black man and the white woman, neither of whom understood the other's language.

Without Tom's disturbing presence, Anne put her heart into the scene. It was a demanding one, as dialogue was limited, and when it was over she knew they had achieved something special.

'No doubt about it, you're good,' Andrew said, his colloquial English startling her. She had convinced herself that he was the half-wild black leader.

'Thanks,' she said, feeling her skin redden. The other actors touched her in congratulation as she returned to her chair.

While she was rehearsing, Miles had slipped out and Sylvie now occupied his chair. She sipped coffee from a paper cup which she held out to Anne. 'Want some?' she asked.

'Thanks, my throat feels parched.'

'It's all the emotion you poured out. You were amazing.'

Sylvie's praise caught Anne off guard. 'Thank you,' she said. Maybe there was a chance they could be friends after all, or if not friends, at least not enemies. 'You look lovely today,' she ventured. It was true. The other woman radiated well-being, although Anne didn't like to guess at the reason.

'I do feel good,' Sylvie agreed. She lowered her head so her long blonde hair curtained her face. 'My feelings tend to show on my face, which is why

I'm an actress, I suppose. I could never hide anything, especially not my latest news.'

Since Sylvie seemed to expect it, Anne asked, 'What news?'

'About Tom and me. Working on the script together last night finally did the trick.'

Anne's throat closed and the woolshed spun around her. She went hot and cold by turns, her stomach churning as she forced herself to ask, 'Tom proposed to you?'

'Isn't it wonderful? It's no surprise, of course, and we're keeping it quiet until the film is completed.' Sylvie bit her full lip apprehensively. 'I had to tell somebody, but you won't say anything to the others, will you? I don't want any special treatment.'

'No, I...I won't,' Anne managed to say. What had made Sylvie choose her, of all people, to confide in? The news hung like a dark cloud over her head. As Sylvie said, it wasn't unexpected. Her mother had warned her, after all. But it still came as a shock to hear that Tom had actually proposed marriage to Sylvie.

The discovery that she was right about Tom provided little consolation. Knowing that his kisses were only a means to an end didn't make her yearn for them any the less. It would be a long time before she ridded herself of the longing to be in his arms.

Whoever said that it was better to have loved and lost had plainly never experienced her torment. It would have been better never to have known the exquisite pleasure-pain of his embraces than to face a future without them.

'Are you all right, Anne?' Sylvie's concerned whisper jolted her back to reality.

'I'm fine,' she insisted. 'The air-conditioning's a little hot in here.'

'I feel quite cool,' Sylvie countered. 'Maybe you're coming down with something.'

Like an acute case of unrequited love, she thought bleakly. Could one really die of a broken heart? It seemed unlikely that the cure would be so simple or painless.

'Miss Fleming? Any chance you might join me up here?'

At Tom's acerbic tone, Anne forced herself out of her chair and walked to the front of the room on shaky legs. She hadn't noticed him returning after his phone call, being too preoccupied with Sylvie's news. She hoped he didn't want to run through one of the love scenes, because she doubted whether she was capable of it right now.

Fortunately, he had another scene in mind. It was a new one in which Katie, the local schoolteacher, defied school policy to teach her pupils about Aboriginal lore and customs.

Anne thought the scene was wonderful and moving. Katie was everything she wished she could be—beautiful, courageous and passionate. In love with Marcus, she was prepared to defy the world to do what she thought was right.

Until this moment, Anne had gladly given Katie full rein, bringing her to vibrant life as if it was the most natural thing in the world. Now, however, Katie was stubbornly locked inside her. Sylvie's news had quenched the flame that gave her life.

Tom's harassed look raked her. 'What's the matter with you, Anne? You're acting like a wind-up doll.'

Probably because she felt like one, she wanted to throw at him. She held her tongue with an effort and stood silent while he railed at her.

Her silence acted like a goad. 'You must believe this is real or no one else in the world will believe it. Do you understand?'

'Yes.'

At the small sound, something snapped inside him. He grabbed her arm and started to hustle her towards the back of the woolshed, barking orders to the others as they went.

'What are you doing? Let go of me!' she protested.

He gave a grim smile of satisfaction. 'Saints be praised, she *is* alive! I was starting to wonder.'

'You haven't answered my question,' she persisted.

'In here.'

He hustled her into an ante-room off what had been the homestead's ballroom. The small room had beautiful cedar window frames and benches. One wall was taken up by a rack of costumes.

Tom pushed her on to one of the benches and began to rifle through the costumes, pulling out and returning several to the rack before he found what he wanted.

'Take those off,' he ordered.

What was the matter with him? She had dressed for rehearsal in a pair of slim-fitting jeans and an old Star Wars T-shirt. When she had chosen it this morning, the irony of the name had amused her,

given the antipathy between her and Sylvie. She
crossed her arms defensively across her breasts. 'Are
you out of your mind?' she demanded.

'Not completely. Are you going to take those
clothes off, or am I going to do it for you?'

She didn't doubt that he was capable of it. 'Very
well, if this is how you get your kicks,' she said
with all the dignity she could muster.

With deliberate slowness, she stood up and teased
the shirt out from the waistband of her jeans. Then
she raised her arms over her head and slid the shirt
up the length of her body. With some satisfaction,
she heard his hissing intake of breath. She peeled
the T-shirt over her head and dropped it to the floor,
then reached behind her.

'You can keep your bra on,' he said. The un-
steadiness in his voice told her she had achieved her
aim. His hands shook slightly as he gestured to the
jeans. 'Those will have to go.'

'Why not?' With a haughty smile, she pushed
the front zip down, taking her time. Let him suffer,
damn him. He was the one who had used her when
he knew all along that he was going to marry Sylvie.
She still didn't know what this charade was all
about, but she intended to make the most of it.

By the time she had wriggled out of her jeans
and stood before him in her lacy bra and panties,
Tom's face was rigid with anger. He looked as if
it was all he could do not to hit her. Or kiss her
into submission, she thought with a flash of regret.
If it hadn't been for Sylvie, she might have broken
down and begged his forgiveness for the way she
was behaving. As it was, she couldn't stop herself
punishing him in the only way open to her.

'Have you finished?' he demanded thickly.

'Yes. I gather you want me to put this on?'

He held out a trailing taffeta gown. She slipped it on, unwillingly conscious that the full, high bust, bell sleeves and hourglass waist flattered her.

Next he handed her a gem straw hat with ribbon band, and she jammed it on her head defiantly. She had intended to unsettle him with her performance, but she was the one whose breathing came unnaturally fast, and she couldn't blame it entirely on the tightly fastened gown. 'Now what?'

'Now you look like Katie Dooley,' he said. 'The station owners keep these costumes for their theme nights. Wearing one should make you feel like Katie as well.'

Remembering his passion for realism, she felt slightly ashamed of her behaviour. 'I see.'

Instead of returning to the woolshed, he led her out to his four-wheel-drive vehicle. 'Get in,' he ordered.

Realism was all very well, but she wasn't going anywhere with him until he explained what he had in mind.

'I've asked the others to meet us at Niagara Dam,' he informed her mildly.

'More realism?'

'If you like.'

Anne didn't like. Wearing the romantic gown drew her thoughts in all sorts of unwelcome directions, but telling him would only reveal how she felt, which was the last thing she wanted him to know. To have him pity her for falling in love with him was more than she could stand.

Emerald Station was located halfway between Kalgoorlie and Niagara, so they reached the dam in half an hour of rugged driving. Anne's bones felt liquid by the time Tom pulled up in a natural red rock amphitheatre. He parked the car under a giant gum tree and got out, then immediately shrugged his shirt off over his head.

Stripped to the waist, his sleekly muscled body glistened like mahogany. When he reached for the zipper of his jeans, she panicked. 'What are you doing?' she asked anxiously.

'I brought Marcus's clothes with me.'

'But Trevor...'

'Trevor telephoned to say he's marooned by floodwaters in Rockhampton. He won't be joining us until we start principal photography.'

It was just her and Tom. Marcus and Katie, she made herself remember. The man who stood before her in riding breeches with coloured shirt and turn-down collar was Marcus, and he loved Katie. There was no Sylvie waiting to wear his ring. Marcus loved her and she loved him.

When he voted to start rehearsing without waiting for the others, her reaction was bitter-sweet. Alone with him in the wilderness, she could let her love for him shine through. It was so easy.

Katie's lines flowed from her with such passion that even Tom looked startled. When he took her in his arms, it was a struggle to remember that Marcus was wooing her, not Tom. Tom belonged to Sylvie.

When Tom-Marcus dragged her closer, forcing a kiss on her chaste mouth—Katie's mouth, she reminded herself frantically—her bones turned to water and fire raced along her veins. She might never have another chance to be in his arms, she told herself. She savoured every enticing fragment of sensation, squirrelling them away against a lonely future.

Katie was a virgin, but there was nothing virginal in the way Anne opened her mouth and invited Tom's tender explorations. In the tightly laced dress, her breasts tingled where they brushed against his chest. Her fingers dug into his back as she confessed her love for him in the only way open to her.

The sound of a car approaching broke the spell. Tom looked shaken as he pulled away from her, as if he sensed the honesty in her performance. He would blame it on the setting and the costume, never suspecting the real cause.

Somehow Anne knew that there would never be a moment as magical as this one. Other rehearsals would have an audience. There was Sylvie to consider. But for this one shining moment, he had been hers, even if he was only playing a part.

He glanced at the car pulling up beside theirs, then looked back at her. 'Anne, I...'

She knew what she had to do. Touching a finger to his lips, she shook her head. 'Not Anne—Katie, remember?'

His arctic gaze became even more wintry as he nodded tautly. 'Katie, of course.'

She was surprised to see Miles emerge from the car alone. 'What happened to the others?' she asked. 'Did they get lost?'

The older actor shook his head. 'I came to find you two. After you left, there was a phone call for Anne. I'm afraid it isn't good news.'

Her heart felt as if someone was squeezing it painfully. She clutched Tom's arm. 'It's Mother, isn't it?'

'She collapsed while out sightseeing. Your friend Sam got her to hospital, and she's in Intensive Care right now.'

The ground tilted under Anne's feet. But for Tom's strong hold on her, she would have fallen. He practically carried her back to the car. 'We'll drive straight to Kalgoorlie,' he said firmly.

'But the rehearsals . . .'

'Hang the rehearsal. You can't be alone at a time like this.'

His strength buoyed her up through the jolting journey back to the city. In a haze of worry and fear, she was barely conscious of the miles passing. Tom had used the radio to contact Kalgoorlie. Her mother was alive but critical. 'I'll get you there in time,' he vowed when she gave a stricken cry.

Alive but critical. Oh, Mother, she agonised, we've shared so much. Why not this? Why am I the last to know that you've been ill?

At the hospital, their costumes drew curious glances, but Tom ignored them as he guided her through the maze of corridors. At last they stood beside the high bed. Her mother was hardly recognisable amid a tangle of tubes and life-support systems. Her face was waxen.

At the sight, Anne gave a strangled cry. 'Mother!'

When Joanna didn't stir, they were led outside, and a doctor explained that her heart had been failing for some time.

'Did she know?' Anne made herself ask.

'She knew. She carried a referral from her own doctor for precisely this eventuality.'

Tears flowed freely down her white face. 'Why didn't she tell me?'

The doctor touched her shoulder. 'There was nothing you could do. She probably didn't want to spoil your last days together.'

Last days? Was there no hope, then? 'I'm afraid not,' the doctor confirmed. 'She may not even wake up.'

The vigil lasted into the night. Like a statue, Anne sat by her mother's bedside, her fingers entwined in the thin, cold ones as if she could will her own life force into Joanna.

Tom never left her side. When the tears came, he held her as she wept against his shoulder. His lips brushed her hair and she clung to him, drawing on his comforting strength. Faced with losing her mother, she knew that only Tom could fill the empty places in her heart. He could give her the reason and the will to go on.

She wanted him more at that moment than ever before, although she felt slightly ashamed of thinking such thoughts at her mother's bedside. But how could she avoid taking stock of her own life at such a time? And these thoughts led her back again and again to how much she needed Tom.

Near dawn, Anne stirred, sensing a change in Joanna. 'Mother?' she whispered.

Joanna's eyelids fluttered open, but she seemed unable to see Anne bending over her. 'Dee?'

This time, the hated name sounded chokingly beautiful. 'It's me, Mother. It's Deanne.' The slender fingers tightened around hers and she clutched her mother's hand to her chest. 'I love you, Mother.'

'Love . . . you too, Dee, always.' The hoarse whisper was barely audible, then Joanna's hand went limp in Anne's. She cradled it against her cheek as the tears poured silently down her face.

Suddenly the room exploded with activity as the nursing staff responded to signals from Joanna's life-support system. Anne was pushed aside while resuscitation attempts were made. They had to try, she supposed, but she knew it was futile. Her mother was gone.

When they confirmed what she already knew, she stumbled into the corridor, supported by Tom's steely grip. Outside, she buried her face against him. 'It's over. I've lost her,' she sobbed.

He stroked her hair over and over. 'You haven't lost her. She's with you as long as you remember her.'

She lifted a tearful face to him. 'I'll always remember her.'

'Then you'll never be without her.'

Shaking with emotion, she clung to him. 'Oh, Tom, I'm so glad you were with me. I couldn't have managed alone.'

He crooked a finger and tilted her head back until their eyes met. 'I had no intention of leaving you to cope alone,' he said gently. 'I'm here for as long as you need me.'

But not forever, she realised bleakly, which was how long she needed him. Losing her mother had shown her how precious he was to her, yet how far beyond her reach. In a daze she saw him speak to the medical staff and to Sam, who had been waiting for news. She accepted her boss's condolences automatically, too numb with grief to remember what was said.

At her side, Tom said gently, 'Come on, I'll drive you home.'

She came back to him slowly. She had no right to keep him with her, however much she needed him. 'You've done too much already,' she protested.

'I haven't even started. Let's go.'

With no strength, or, for that matter, no real wish to argue, Anne let him steer her back to the car. The streets were dark and silent, and her bachelor quarters felt unutterably lonely when he opened the door with her key.

Feeling lost, she stood in the middle of the floor, plucking at the trailing skirt of her period costume. Making any sort of decision seemed beyond her.

He took a look at her face and made it for her. 'Get changed and throw some things into a bag. You're coming back to the hotel with me.'

Her numb brain fought to deal with the instruction. There was a reason why she couldn't go with him. 'Won't Sylvie mind?' she asked as the reason penetrated the fog in her mind.

'You're not still worried about holding up rehearsals, are you? I assure you Sylvie will understand.'

He seemed sure of himself, she thought disjointedly. What a wonderful, secure relationship he must have with Sylvie if she wouldn't mind him taking another woman to his hotel suite, even if he was only being a friend in need.

Guiding her to her wardrobe, he helped her to select some clothes. What they were hardly registered; she had stopped feeling anything an hour ago.

'Shall I help you to change?' Tom asked.

It was tempting to say yes and have him help her out of the costume. But she had imposed enough. There was a limit to Sylvie's capacity to understand. 'No, thanks, I can manage,' she insisted.

'Very well. I'll take your bag to the car while you dress.'

She shed Katie with the dress, dropping her on to the bed like the empty shell she was. It was fitting that Katie was empty. She was like Anne herself, empty and alone. She had no one—not Joanna, and certainly not Tom.

When she took too long emerging, he came back to find her crying again. She had managed to change into black pants and a grey linen top and was slipping her feet into low-heeled pumps when she caught sight of her mother's picture on her dresser.

'It's all right, cry if you want to,' Tom urged when he saw what she was looking at.

'I'm s-sorry,' she gulped. 'I c-can't seem to s-stop.'

His crooked finger traced the path of a tear down her cheek. 'Don't apologise for loving, Anne. It's the greatest tribute you can pay your mother.'

She managed a shaky smile. 'Thanks for understanding.'

His arms came around her in a quick hug. 'Don't mention it. After all, what are friends for?'

CHAPTER TEN

THERE was no longer any point in pretending. Newspapers all over the country had reported Joanna's collapse and her daughter's rush to her bedside. Afterwards it was even worse, with reporters following her everywhere.

During the first nightmarish days, Anne blessed Tom for whisking her away to the hotel. It took the media some time to track her down, and by then she was ready to cope with the onslaught.

'Who'd have thought that sweet exterior concealed a secret past?' Nancy marvelled as they sat in Anne's hotel room, sharing coffee.

Sam had sent her to see if there was anything Anne needed. When she saw that company was the most pressing requirement, dear practical Nancy had stayed to provide it, with Sam's blessing.

How could she have doubted that Nancy was a true friend? Beyond a healthy curiosity about Anne's family history, she hadn't changed. She was as forthright and friendly as ever.

'It's the first time my exterior's been called sweet,' Anne retorted, grimacing.

'You know what I mean. Why didn't you say something? I wouldn't have told anyone.'

'I know, and I love you for it, Nance. But if you'd spent as much time as I have living in someone else's shadow, you'd do the same.'

'I suppose so. Look, if you need anything at all...'

'Thanks, but time is the only thing that will heal me now. I don't know what I would have done without you and Greg—and Sam, of course.'

'And Tom Callander,' Nancy contributed. 'He guards you from the media like a bear defending its cub. Where is he now, by the way?'

A shadow passed across Anne's eyes. 'He went to Emerald Station on film business.' To see Sylvie, her traitorous heart added. Aloud, she said, 'I feel so guilty, keeping all those people on stand-by because of me.'

Nancy grinned. 'I don't imagine they mind having a paid holiday at Emerald. It's the most luxurious tourist farm in the state.'

Anne doubted whether Sylvie would agree. She was the most likely reason why Tom had hurried back. No amount of luxury would make up for Tom's absence.

So she was doubly surprised when he returned that afternoon and announced that he was accompanying her back to Perth. 'There's no need, I can manage,' she insisted.

'You won't have to—I'll be there.'

He had left Andrew in charge of the group at Emerald Station, he told her when she tried to argue. They would manage well enough until he got back.

It was on the tip of her tongue to ask what Sylvie thought, then she recalled how angry he had become the last time she had mentioned the other woman. He must have discussed his plans with Sylvie and received her blessing.

Anne certainly welcomed his support. Her mother's affairs were complicated and there was a lot to be done beyond the agonising details of the funeral itself.

How she would have survived it without Tom, she didn't know. He always seemed to be nearby, whether it was in watery sunshine at Joanna's graveside, or afterwards when the lawyers' meetings grew endless.

Anne lost count of the days, but she knew he was staying in Perth far longer than she had any right to expect. 'I can't let you keep playing nursemaid to me,' she insisted when he arrived at Joanna's house one evening.

He gave an exaggerated sigh. 'Still the wrong response, Anne. I thought you'd learned by now.'

A wintry smile brightened her pale face. 'Thank you, Tom, for everything. You've been wonderful.'

'You make it sound as if it's over.'

A feeling of desolation gripped her. 'It has to be. Sooner or later I have to stand on my own feet.'

'Agreed, but there's no hurry, is there?'

'What about the cast? I can't keep you from them for much longer.'

'It's only been a couple of weeks,' he reminded her. 'Although it probably feels longer to you.'

It felt like a lifetime, Anne acknowledged wearily. She felt as if she had aged years since Miles had brought them the news at Niagara Dam. She had been in Tom's arms then, being kissed by him more poignantly than she had ever been kissed before.

He wasn't kissing you, he was kissing Katie Dooley, she reminded herself angrily. When would she learn to separate the two? Tom didn't seem to find it difficult.

'Tired?' he asked when she passed a hand across her eyes.

'A bit. Going through Mother's things was harder than I anticipated.'

'Never mind, it's over now. The estate agents will take care of the rest.' His hand rested lightly on her shoulder. 'You've held up brilliantly.'

She dropped dark lashes over brimming eyes. 'I don't feel brilliant. I feel as if I'm constantly on the verge of going to pieces.'

'But you haven't gone to pieces, and you won't,' he said with mock severity. 'Your mother would be proud of the way you've carried on.'

'What a lovely thing to say. But I couldn't have done it without you, Tom.'

He rolled his eyes heavenwards. 'I think she's finally got the message.'

Anne smiled for the first time in days. 'I mean it. Thank you.' On impulse, she lifted herself on tiptoe and kissed him gently. She had meant to kiss his cheek, but he turned his head at the wrong moment and her lips caught the corner of his mouth.

Before she knew what was happening, she was in his arms and his lips were devouring hers hungrily. Because it was so unexpected, she had no time to prepare, and found herself kissing him back with all the pent-up desire in her.

The room spun crazily as her fingers curved convulsively around his shoulders. Tendrils of desire wound their way around her core until she closed her eyes in ecstasy.

When he put her away from him she could only think she had disappointed him in some way. But the look in his eyes belied any such notion. He wanted her as much as she wanted him.

The discovery went to her head like strong wine, and her heart sang. Then she remembered why it was wrong for them to behave this way. 'I'm sorry, I didn't mean . . .'

'I shouldn't have——' he said at the same moment, and dragged stiff fingers through his hair. 'I didn't mean to take advantage of you.'

He had been apart from Sylvie for too long, she thought bleakly, and had realised it in time, long before Anne herself. Her cheeks burned. How could she have let herself go so completely, knowing he belonged to someone else?

'Would you like to go out for dinner?' he asked, his tone oddly formal after the recent intimacy.

Sending him away made more sense than torturing herself with crumbs, she thought savagely. Go ahead, do it now. He'll be gone before long anyway. But her throat closed on the words. 'All right,' she whispered miserably. 'I'll get my jacket.'

He took her to a family-run Italian bistro where they ate pasta and salad and crusty bread heavy with garlic. There was wine too, a fruity Chianti which seemed to disappear from her glass with surprising speed. It was just as well she wasn't driving home.

Yet she wasn't intoxicated, she knew. The wine had merely dulled the emotional knife-edge on which she'd been poised since . . . since meeting Tom, she realised. Nothing had been ordinary since then. If she could have charted her days lately, they'd be full of jagged peaks and plunging troughs, each one lower than the one before.

No wonder she had weakened in Tom's arms. It was a miracle she functioned rationally at all.

He was strangely quiet as he drove her home. Anne longed to ask what was troubling him. He shouldn't feel bad about kissing her. In her vulnerability, she had invited it, so she was more at fault than he was. Yet she couldn't regret the moment, even if he did. It was too precious for regrets.

At her front door, her tension escalated, piercing the haze of wine and tiredness that enveloped her. Tom had locked his car when they left it, as if he intended to stay a while. She only noticed because the habit was at odds with country behaviour. Only a city person routinely locked a car around here.

At the threshold, she spun around, blocking the entrance. 'Goodnight, Tom,' she said. 'It was a lovely evening.'

He loomed over her, looking more formidable than usual in the silvery light. 'It isn't over yet.'

Why was he doing this to her? 'It has to be,' she appealed.

'That's your conscience speaking,' he said, his voice huskily caressing in the stillness. 'Does your heart want me to go as well?'

It was a cruel question, but it demanded honesty. 'No.'

'Then I won't go.'

He steered her inside and shut the door behind them, before snapping on a table lamp. The low light accentuated the planes and hollows of his face, giving it a devilish cast. 'Come here, Anne.'

His open arms beckoned and everything in her longed to surrender to them. But it was wrong. 'I can't.'

'So you keep saying. Yet you want to—I can feel it.'

She licked her dry lips. 'We can't always have what we want, can we?'

'Not always, if there's a good reason for holding back.'

'Such as a fiancée?' she demanded, pain making her voice ragged.

He lowered his eyes. 'You mean Sylvie?'

Why was he torturing her like this? 'Of course I mean Sylvie,' she snapped. 'How many fiancées do you have, for goodness' sake?'

He lifted his head and looked straight at her. 'None.'

Of course not, because it wasn't official yet, she remembered Sylvie saying. 'You're still not—not free,' she stammered, suddenly unsure of herself. If he wasn't officially engaged, did she still have a duty to send him away? Dear heaven, did she even have the strength?

'I'm as free to follow my heart as you are,' he assured her, making a crossing motion over his chest. 'Unless you're looking for excuses. Or——' he drew a rasping breath '—unless I'm wrong about us and you *want* me to leave?'

How could he think such a thing? Everything in her cried out for him to stay. 'I don't want you to go,' she whispered. 'Stay with me, Tom, please?'

No matter what sort of woman it made her, she wanted this one night to remember him by. In her wildest dreams, she couldn't imagine another man making her feel as he did, so it would have to last her for a long, long time.

His breath warmed her cheek as he approached and she gasped with pleasure as his kisses feathered her forehead, face and neck. By the time he found her mouth, her back was arched in ecstasy.

Under the curtain of her hair, his hand was warm on her nape, while his other hand pressed into the small of her back, drawing her close to him. With a cry of surrender she linked both hands behind his head and closed her eyes. Don't think, feel, she ordered herself. Tonight, he isn't promised to anyone but you.

Her eyes flew open as he slid an arm under her knees and lifted her effortlessly. 'What are you doing?' she whispered.

He covered her face with tiny kisses as he carried her to the bedroom. 'Don't ask silly questions.'

It *was* a silly question, she found out moments later when he slid her upright at the bedside and undid the crystal buttons of her dress. By the time the silky fabric lay in a black cloud around her feet, she could hardly breathe. Her bra floated after the dress, and he cupped her breasts in skilled hands, then bent to worship the creamy mounds with his mouth.

She had never felt so beautiful or so beloved as he dropped to his knees and continued the exquisite onslaught across her stomach and thighs, sliding her lace panties down to join the dress.

With a throaty cry, he stood up and stripped off his own shirt and trousers, dropping them haphazardly on top of hers. While he undressed, she lay back and cupped a hand behind her head, feasting her eyes on his magnificence as it was swiftly revealed to her.

She trembled with expectancy as he stretched full-length beside her, his limbs lean and brown in contrast to her slender paleness. He seemed to find the contrast fascinating, and tremors shook her as he ran a hand down her stomach.

'You're so beautiful,' he murmured, encircling her engorged nipple with his tongue. She gave a soft gasp as his hand invaded her centre, the caresses driving her to mindless heavenly excitement. The lamp painted them in glowing gold, and by its light Anne saw that his passion more than matched her own.

With wondering fingers, she stroked him, and his breath hissed from between clenched teeth. But when she took her hand away he guided her back, letting her love him with her touch until tremors swept through him and she knew it was time.

'Love me, please,' she pleaded, opening herself to him, every reservation banished from her mind in the exquisite joy of his possession.

As he drove her ever harder and higher, it crossed her mind that there could be a child. They had done nothing to prevent it. The thought exploded through her in joyous waves. If there was, it would be the greatest gift he could give her. When he was gone from her, she would still have a precious part of him for all time.

The knowledge filled her with joy which she gave to him in turn, in passionate abandon, until a cry of triumph tore the air. It was only as her breathing slowed that she realised the cry had been her own.

* * *

After Tom had fallen asleep, Anne lay awake, too languorous to get up and turn off the lamp. By its golden glow, she watched him sleeping, and drank in the sight, hoarding it for the future when he was married to Sylvie.

Married to Sylvie. She stifled a sob. How could she think of him in the other woman's arms after what they had just shared?

You knew the score, she told herself severely. She hadn't allowed for how she would feel afterwards. Loving Tom was like trying to eat one chocolate from a box. Vowing you wouldn't didn't stop you from wanting the rest. And how she wanted the rest.

Her hand strayed to her flat stomach. Would it swell with his child one day soon? She hoped so with everything in her, because it would be all she had. She could rationalise this one night because he wasn't actually engaged yet, but once Sylvie wore his ring it would be over. Anne had seen too much unhappiness in the film industry to want to undermine Tom's marriage.

He stirred and looked at her, his hands seeking hers. 'Can't sleep?'

'I was thinking.'

He propped himself up on one elbow and traced a pattern across her stomach. Catching his hand, she pressed it to her lips. 'Keep doing that and I won't be able to think at all.'

He gave a throaty growl. 'Not a bad idea.'

'You're insatiable.'

'You don't know the half of it.'

She could hardly believe they could make love again so quickly. Tom seemed to have endless re-

serves of energy. The peak he took her to seemed
higher than the last, as he loved her, if anything,
more deeply and fully than before. Her skin
glistened and her chest heaved as she came slowly
back to earth.

Her thighs ached, but wisps of pleasure spiralled
through her as she lay beside him. She felt languid
but truly alive for the first time. 'Where do you get
your stamina from?' she asked in wonder.

'Good living and a clear conscience,' he ticked
them off on his fingers. 'Or maybe you do something to me.' He kissed her lightly. 'That's it—
you're a witch and you have me under a spell. I'm
yours till the end of time.'

If only it was true, she thought as a wintry feeling
swept through her. 'Don't,' she pleaded on a half-
sob. Although she blinked hard to hold them back,
two rivers of tears slid down her cheeks.

Tom brushed them away with the back of his
hand. 'This can't go on,' he said, his voice rough.
'You and I need to talk.'

Miles was right—Tom could be wonderfully per-
suasive when he wanted to be, Anne discovered that
night. Maybe she was hearing what she wanted to
hear, but she was glad he wasn't selling the Sydney
Opera House. She might well have decided to buy
it.

'You're looking well,' said Miles, dropping a kiss
on her cheek. 'I've kept your seat at the woolshed
warm for you.'

'I don't deserve you,' she said, smiling at the
circle of people surrounding her. 'Thanks for
sending the wreath; it was thoughtful.'

Miles shook his head. 'We were only sorry we couldn't do more.'

'Your calls and letters were enough. They helped keep me going.'

Tension rippled through her as Sylvie approached, but it was only to kiss the air near her cheek. 'It's a shame you had to come back,' Sylvie told her.

Miles gasped. 'Sylvie!'

'I mean because we were having such a great holiday,' Sylvie said, smiling sweetly. 'Now we'll have to get back to work.'

'Speaking of which,' Tom interrupted, 'I hate to break up the welcome home party, but we have some catching up to do. I want a complete run-through of the wedding scene in the woolshed at two, in costume.'

Sylvie pouted. 'Surely you don't expect us to dress up for a simple read-through?'

'I thought the instruction was clear enough,' Tom said with a thread of steel in his voice. 'The costumes will give everyone a real feel for this scene. It isn't a read-through, it's a wedding, understood?'

There was a chorus of agreement, although Sylvie went away muttering under her breath about people who couldn't tell reality from fantasy.

Anne watched her go with a heavy heart. Her earlier animosity towards Sylvie had vanished, replaced by a dragging sadness. Did Sylvie suspect that she and Tom were lovers? Anne felt as if she wore the fact like a brand and had half expected Sylvie to confront her with her guilt.

No one had commented on the fact that she was Joanna Flame's daughter, she also noticed. Tom must have warned them to leave the subject alone. She was grateful. The hurt of her mother's death was still too raw to endure public probing. She had also demonstrated that the part of Katie Dooley was hers by right of talent, she thought defiantly. They couldn't accuse her of pulling strings to get it.

She was glad she had spent some time studying the script so that her lines were still fresh in her mind. A quick glance at the wedding scene refreshed her memory, so she needed only to get into costume ready to rehearse.

There was chaos in the room off the ballroom as the actors tried on gowns and frock coats. Anne didn't have to look far for her dress. There was only one bridal gown, and it hung in solitary splendour against a wall.

'It's gorgeous. It looks like an heirloom,' she gasped as she fingered the full-length gown with its high, lace-trimmed bodice and full skirt trimmed with hand embroidery and a deep flounce around the hem. The veil was gossamer-light with a crown of silk flowers.

'It is an heirloom. The owners of Emerald Station gave us special permission to use it,' Tom said, hearing her exclamation. 'I checked the fit. It should be perfect.'

He looked stunningly handsome in Marcus's wedding clothes of plum-coloured breeches, cream waistcoat over white ruffled shirt, and deep blue morning coat.

'My, what a splendid couple you make,' Sylvie muttered as she went past clutching her white muslin bridesmaid's dress and wide-brimmed hat trimmed with feathers.

Tom doffed his top hat to her. 'Kind of you to say so, Sylvie. I happen to agree.'

'Stop it, you're only making things worse,' Anne hissed at him as she adjusted the frothy veil in the mirror. It trailed almost to the floor.

He looked at her without a trace of embarrassment. 'Sylvie's an adult. I don't need to wrap her in cotton wool.'

Anne felt her face flame. 'But there's no need to rub in the fact that you and I ... that we ...' Her voice failed her.

He took her arm. 'You're the one who's drawing attention to us.'

She was, she saw in horror. The others gave them furtive looks as they dressed. Anne made an effort to calm herself, but it was difficult, given the squadron of butterflies that were performing an air show inside her.

Tom looked around. 'Everyone ready?'

'Almost everyone,' said Andrew. His skin looked blacker than usual against his costume of cream breeches and waistcoat and dark morning coat. His character's trademark black beard provided even more of a contrast.

In the script, it was one of Katie's triumphs that she had persuaded the wild Aborigine to attend the wedding. One of the guests was supposed to slip away and betray him to the troopers.

Tom looked around, frowning in irritation. 'Who's missing?'

'Our preacher is marooned with Trevor up in Rockhampton.'

'Never mind. Miles has agreed to read his lines for now.'

Anne was glad. Miles looked every inch the country preacher in his formal clothes, and his Shakespearian training would stand him in good stead, although his main task was to read the traditional wedding service.

Someone had decked the woolshed out as a chapel, she noticed with pleasure, when they assembled there for the rehearsal.

'This is carrying realism too far,' Sylvie grumbled. 'Next thing you know, they'll be expecting a honeymoon.'

Did she suspect that they had already pre-empted the honeymoon? Anne wondered, feeling a pang. Despite her best efforts and Tom's advice, she couldn't make herself feel good about Sylvie. If the roles were reversed, she couldn't stand to watch Tom take another woman as his bride, even on film.

Tom gave orders and the rehearsal started, giving her no time for further self-recrimination. First, she had to hide Coyle among the wedding guests, pretending that he was a black tracker employed by the mine.

The script called for the troopers to become suspicious, forcing Marcus to start the wedding before the guests could be investigated.

An organ wheezed into life. It was a recording, but it sounded convincingly ancient in the woolshed setting. Goose-bumps ran up and down Anne's spine as she readied herself for the walk to the altar where Miles waited with Tom.

In a dream, she floated down the aisle between the chairs. The woolshed had become a chapel, and ahead of her, haloed in light, was the man she loved. Her radiant expression demanded no acting skill at all.

Tom's eyes softened as he watched her. Was he seeing Katie Dooley at that moment? It hardly mattered, since she and Katie were one and the same. Her steps quickened as she moved towards him.

'Dearly beloved, we are gathered together here...' Miles intoned in a clarion voice. His trained voice lent new richness and meaning to the traditional ceremony. Only when he called upon Marcus and Katie to make their vows did he falter. He gave a spluttering cough and began again in a much lower tone.

Tom looked lovingly at Anne and his fingers twined with hers. 'I will,' he said in a voice like velvet.

Miles was still having difficulty with his speech. Anne's, 'I will,' was pronounced in a clear, ringing voice, but for the rest of the vows their voices dropped, as if the three of them were alone in the room.

Suddenly Miles recovered his voice. 'I now pronounce that they be man and wife together. You may kiss the bride.'

With infinite slowness, Tom lifted the gossamer veil that hid her face. Her eyes shone wetly as they gazed into his. Dropping his hands to her shoulders, he drew her closer and his lips melded with hers. They held the pose for a long moment until Anne grew dizzy with lack of air, then he released her.

A burst of applause greeted the end of the scene. 'Sorry about the voice,' Miles said on a slight cough. 'I don't know what happened there.'

Tom smiled at Anne. 'It doesn't matter. I think it went very well, don't you?'

'Shall we run through it again?' she asked, feeling shy as she realised he still held her hand.

He shook his head. 'Let's not try to improve on perfection.'

'If you can capture that same magic on film, you should win every award in the book,' Andrew said generously. 'You almost convinced me it was a real ceremony.'

'I told you the costumes would make the difference.'

'I still don't see why the rest of us had to dress up, since we don't have any lines in this scene,' Sylvie complained.

She was even less happy when the owner of Emerald Station, who was one of the 'witnesses', insisted on taking pictures of them in their wedding finery. 'It will be wonderful publicity for the station,' he said. 'I hope you don't mind.'

'Not at all,' Tom assured him. He ushered the group outside, where they assembled in traditional wedding poses for the photographer. Against the backdrop of the woolshed and the Australian bush, Anne had a sense of being transported back in time. All that was missing was the preacher.

'Thanks, everyone. You can change for the next scene,' said Tom when enough photographs had been taken.

He put an arm around Anne's waist. 'I'm sorry about making you work. You look as if you should be climbing aboard a horse and carriage for your honeymoon.'

'Realism can be carried *too* far,' Sylvie said, overhearing him.

He gave a heavy sigh. 'You could be right.'

He went back inside the woolshed, and Sylvie watched him go, her expression smug. 'I wouldn't want him getting ideas about this—nor you either,' she added, shooting Anne a venomous look.

Anne smiled wistfully. 'A rehearsal is hardly a wedding, is it?'

Slightly mollified, Sylvie nodded. 'It's true, and I dare say Tom will find the practice useful for the future, if you know what I mean?'

Yes, she did know, Anne thought uncomfortably. She wondered what Sylvie would say if she knew that Tom and Anne had been practising already.

CHAPTER ELEVEN

'THIS is the most exciting thing to happen in this town in years!' Nancy enthused as she lifted a glass of champagne off the tray of a passing waiter. 'It was wonderful of Tom to bring the première to Kalgoorlie.'

'The film is entitled *Kalgoorlie Gold*,' Anne reminded her with a laugh. 'The main thing is you liked it, didn't you?'

Nancy's eyes sparkled. 'Are you kidding? When you—I mean, Katie—married Marcus, I almost cried. It was just like a real wedding.'

'We had plenty of practice at it,' Anne commented, remembering the first time they had rehearsed the scene in the woolshed at Emerald Station.

It seemed like so long ago since that day. In between were months of hard work making the film, then all the difficulties of post-production, when the miles of film were edited into the finished form. Where something had gone wrong, such as a plane flying over a supposedly colonial setting, the anachronism had had to be painted out frame by frame.

But the film was finished at last, and, judging from the reception it had received from the invited audience, it was going to be a success.

If only her mother could be here to see it, Anne thought. She was sure Joanna was proud of her, wherever she was now.

'Such a long face on a special night,' Sam said with a hint of reproof in his voice. 'You must know you were terrific.'

'Well, everybody laughed and cried in all the right places, so it can't be too bad.' Anne sobered suddenly. 'I was thinking of Mother, wishing she could be here.'

'I'm sure she's proud of you,' he said, echoing her thoughts. 'I know we all are.'

It was true. Although most people knew about her mother by now, their treatment of her hadn't changed. With typical country openness, they valued her for herself, she realised belatedly, wishing she'd had the courage to trust them in the beginning.

Only one thing had changed. Nancy no longer paired her off with awful men. 'They don't deserve you,' she explained. 'A man like Tom Callander's much more your style.'

Automatically her eyes sought him out in the crowd. He was easily the best-looking man in the room, his broad frame elegant in a perfectly tailored dinner-jacket. She watched him hungrily as he mounted the podium and adjusted the microphone. Watching him had become a bad habit over the last few months. She wondered if it would ever wear off.

'Ladies and gentlemen, thank you for attending this première,' he began. 'I'm pleased to tell you that, with the matching donation promised from Callander Films, the budget for the drop-in centre has been reached. The mayor will turn the first sod tomorrow. He's also asked me to tell you that they've decided on a name for the centre. It will be known as the Joanna Flame Youth Centre. Since her daughter is one of your own and worked her charming tail off to make this project a reality, I'm sure you agree it's appropriate.'

A lump swelled in Anne's throat as people crowded around to congratulate her. 'My mother couldn't ask for a nicer memorial,' she said in a choked voice.

A high-pitched giggle drew her attention. 'I suppose you're happy now, with your mother's name plastered all over town?'

'It was Tom's idea, not mine,' she said stiffly, telling herself that Sylvie didn't mean it. It was the champagne talking.

Sylvie's almond eyes narrowed. 'I'll bet. As if it was talent and not connections that got you *my* part.'

'You don't know what you're saying,' Anne defended herself.

'Don't I? I suppose I'm wrong about you sleeping with Tom too, when the truth's written all over your face?'

'No, you're not wrong,' Tom said. His voice cut through the hubbub with the force of a whipcrack. 'As far as I know, there's no harm in a man sleeping with his wife.'

Sylvie's jaw dropped open. 'His *what*?'

He moved to Anne's side and put an arm around her waist. 'You heard correctly. Anne and I were married during rehearsals for *Kalgoorlie Gold*.'

'The rehearsal!' she hissed as light dawned. 'I knew there was something odd about it. You went to too much trouble for a mere read-through. But wait a minute.' Her brow wrinkled in confusion.

'How can you be legally married? There was no minister at the rehearsal.'

'No, but there was a civil marriage celebrant,' Miles Davidson said on a note of triumph. He grinned broadly as he joined the group. 'Every actor needs a second string to his bow. Mine is performing marriages.'

'Your fit of laryngitis during the ceremony—you were saying their real names, weren't you? And then *you* said your vows so quietly that we didn't hear your names...'

Miles nodded. 'It was devious, but it worked. Of course the witnesses had to be in on the secret as well.'

Sylvie looked as if she had been poleaxed, and the hum of comment grew to a roar as the guests rushed to congratulate the happy couple.

Nancy looked smug. 'This is one secret I'm glad you didn't keep from me. I'd have killed you if you hadn't shared it with me.'

'I had to tell somebody,' Anne said. Now that the secret was out her body felt light, as if she was floating. 'I didn't want anyone else knowing until my performance had been judged on its own merit.'

'Which it has been, so you can stop worrying,' Nancy told her firmly. 'What will your next role be?'

Anne's shy glance found Tom. 'Wife and mother,' she insisted. 'Tom assures me I won't have time for much else.'

Nancy's dismay increased. 'Will you leave Kalgoorlie for good, then?'

'Only until Tom's new studio is off and running,' Anne assured her friend. 'Tom has bought some land north of Kalgoorlie where he can have a quiet place to write. So I'll be able to help out at the drop-in centre whenever we're in town.'

'We should be spending quite a bit of time at our property,' he contributed. 'In about nine months' time.'

With a squeal of delight, Nancy flung her arms around her friend. 'I *knew* it! Nobody eats ice-cream with pickles unless they're pregnant.'

Anne made a face. 'I didn't think it was such a giveaway. It seemed perfectly normal at the time.'

'At last I'll be able to babysit for you for a change.'

Tom took Anne's arm. 'It's late, and you look tired, Mrs Callander.'

How marvellous to hear it said publicly. She had rehearsed it aloud in private many times since their wedding, and now there was no need to keep it a secret any longer. 'I'm not *too* tired,' she denied, watching the response that flamed in his eyes.

Keeping their secret had meant a good deal of comings and goings under cover of darkness, trysts in out-of-the-way places, and plain old subterfuge. Snatching moments together here and there had given their marriage added sparkle.

Nevertheless, Anne was relieved that the truth was out. An illicit affair, however exciting, couldn't compare with the bliss of walking upstairs together, hand in hand, not caring who saw them.

'You could have picked a more gentle way to break the news to Sylvie,' she chided, when they were alone in the honeymoon suite.

'She wasn't being gentle with you,' he said. 'I gave her what she deserved.'

'But you knew she had her eye on you. She must be dreadfully embarrassed about all her hints that you were going to marry her after you'd finished this film.'

'I've already explained that it was her own idea,' Tom reminded her. 'I went out with her for a while before I met you, and it proved to me, at least, how incompatible we were, except as friends. She didn't really expect me to marry her. She just wanted to rattle you into giving up the part she wanted for herself.'

How blind could a man be? Couldn't he look in a mirror and see why Sylvie was so attracted to him? It wasn't only the role she wanted, but Tom himself, Anne was sure. It must have hurt her terribly to discover that she had been fooling herself all along.

'How could I look at another woman after meeting you?' he asked. 'You're everything I ever dreamed of, but never thought I'd be lucky enough to find.'

'You're taking the words out of my mouth,' she protested, before he silenced her by kissing her passionately.

'Be quiet, woman! I'm the director of this production.'

Her muffled laughter vibrated against his mouth and she freed herself long enough to say, 'Thank you, Tom, for everything.' Especially for loving me, she added inwardly.

He crushed her to him with a muffled oath. 'No, this time, thank *you*.'

Her glance went to his face. 'For what?'

'For having the courage to marry me in such a crazy fashion. For making my life complete. I love you, Anne.'

'And I love you too,' she murmured dreamily. 'Love is like gold, so elusive, yet so rare and precious when you find it.'

'And we've found the mother-lode,' he said huskily. 'It should last us a lifetime at least.'

Her starry-eyed look told him she couldn't agree more.

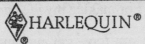

HARLEQUIN®

Don't miss these Harlequin favorites by some of our
most distinguished authors! And now you can receive a
discount by ordering two or more titles!

HT#25657	PASSION AND SCANDAL by Candace Schuler	$3.25 U.S $3.75 CAN.	☐ ☐
HP#11787	TO HAVE AND TO HOLD by Sally Wentworth	$3.25 U.S. $3.75 CAN.	☐ ☐
HR#03385	THE SISTER SECRET by Jessica Steele	$2.99 U.S. $3.50 CAN	☐ ☐
HS#70634	CRY UNCLE by Judith Arnold	$3.75 U.S. $4.25 CAN.	☐ ☐
HI#22346	THE DESPERADO by Patricia Rosemoor	$3.50 U.S. $3.99 CAN	☐ ☐
HAR#16610	MERRY CHRISTMAS, MOMMY by Muriel Jensen	$3.50 U.S. $3.99 CAN.	☐ ☐
HH#28895	THE WELSHMAN'S WAY by Margaret Moore	$4.50 U.S. $4.99 CAN.	☐ ☐

(limited quantities available on certain titles)

AMOUNT	$
DEDUCT: 10% DISCOUNT FOR 2+ BOOKS	$
POSTAGE & HANDLING ($1.00 for one book, 50¢ for each additional)	$
APPLICABLE TAXES*	$
TOTAL PAYABLE	$

(check or money order—please do not send cash)

To order, complete this form and send it, along with a check or money order
for the total above, payable to Harlequin Books, to: **In the U.S.:** 3010 Walden
Avenue, P.O. Box 9047, Buffalo, NY 14269-9047; **In Canada:** P.O. Box 613,
Fort Erie, Ontario, L2A 5X3.

Name: _____

Address: _____ City: _____

State/Prov.: _____ Zip/Postal Code: _____

*New York residents remit applicable sales taxes.
 Canadian residents remit applicable GST and provincial taxes.   HBACK-OD3

Look us up on-line at: http://www.romance.net

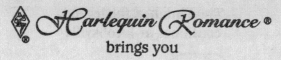

This summer, the legend
continues in Jacobsville

Diana Palmer

A LONG, TALL TEXAN SUMMER

Three **BRAND-NEW** short stories

This summer, Silhouette brings readers a special
collection for Diana Palmer's LONG, TALL TEXANS
fans. Diana has rounded up three **BRAND-NEW**
stories of love Texas-style, all set in Jacobsville,
Texas. Featuring the men you've grown to love from
this wonderful town, this collection is a must-have
for all fans!

*They grow 'em tall in the saddle in Texas—and
they've got love and marriage on their minds!*

Don't miss this collection of original Long, Tall Texans
stories...available in June at your favorite retail outlet.